MW00488757

A COP'S EYES

VERTICAL.

A COP'S EYES

Gaku Yakumaru

Translated by Jan Mitsuko Cash

VERTICAL.

First published in Japan in 2012 by Kodansha Ltd., Tokyo.
Publication rights for this English edition arranged
through Kodansha Ltd., Tokyo.

Published by Vertical, Inc., New York, 2016

Originally published in Japanese as *Keiji no Manazashi* in 2011
and reissued in paperback in 2012

ISBN 978-1-941220-57-3

Manufactured in the United States of America

First Edition

Vertical, Inc.
451 Park Avenue South, 7th Floor
New York, NY 10016

www.vertical-inc.com

CONTENTS

A COP'S EYES

Black Record

Shinichi Koide was loitering around the front shopping street of Otsuka station.

It was already getting dark. When he saw a lighted bar sign, a strong temptation to have a drink came rushing to him, but he decided against it. If he drank now, he would likely drink himself into a stupor.

Since half a year ago, Shinichi had been working at an *izakaya* pub in Ikebukuro, but he'd just been dismissed by the manager.

It happened right when he thought he was finally getting used to the work. He'd heard that business hadn't been good lately. Even so, he resented that out of all the many employees, he was the one laid off. Why, when he'd worked harder at this job than any other? When he pressed the manager for a reason, the mealy-mouthed answer was that times were hard and it couldn't be helped.

When Shinichi saw the manager's expression, he sensed it. There was only one reason. The manager had gotten wind of his past.

It was always like this. No matter how many times he tried to start his life over, his past, his black record, always got in the way.

The manager said they'd postpone the dismissal for a month so that he could find a different job in that time. Shinichi had kicked over a nearby chair and rushed out of the pub. Since then, he'd been walking aimlessly.

He passed by the front of a gaming arcade and stopped.

When he looked at the crane game sitting outside, the prizes in it were new. They were dolls of a rabbit character called Momo-chan that was popular among children.

Thinking of bringing one home to Haruna, he put in a hundred-yen coin.

He focused on the dolls piled in the case and fixed his aim. When he pressed the button with perfect timing, the crane grabbed the doll in his sights and dropped it down the chute.

Today had sucked, but at least for this game, the gods hadn't abandoned him. Shinichi was great at it. He'd improved from playing time and time again to get gifts for Haruna, his niece whom he lived with.

He put the vinyl doll into his jacket pocket and headed to his East Ikebukuro apartment, which was a twenty-minute walk away.

In a dim alley of the residential area, he spotted a small figure wearing a school backpack.

"Mai," he called to her back, and the girl's shoulders twitched and she stopped in her tracks. Mai Yokose slowly turned around with a tense expression.

Calling out to her in a desolate alley must have startled her.

"Haruna's big brother," Mai said, her face relaxing.

She seemed to think Shinichi was Haruna's brother, but he didn't bother to correct her. It was better than being called an uncle.

"You're not with Haruna today?" Shinichi asked while walking with Mai.

Mai and Haruna were classmates in the fourth grade and also went to the same cram school. But when he saw the two walking together, they hardly looked the same age. Mai was taller than Haruna, and unlike Haruna, who was always noisy, she lacked the characteristic bright perkiness of a child. Perhaps her large, somehow melancholic eyes were what made her seem more mature than her age.

"Yeah. I had some shopping to do, so we said bye partway."

Mai and her father lived together in a nearby house. It was a fairly impressive one. According to Haruna, who'd gone there to play, they had a large TV, an expensive-looking video camera, and such. Shinichi didn't know what the father did, but as the landlord of the apartment building that Shinichi and Haruna lived in, the family couldn't be struggling.

"Don't tell me you're the one who makes dinner?" Shinichi said, glancing at the bag of groceries hanging from her right hand.

"Not every day, but sometimes..."

"Good for you. I wish Haruna would follow your example."

Haruna lived with her single mother, but he'd never seen her help with the housework. Shinichi's older sister, Naoko, often scolded Haruna to at least clean up the messes she made.

Near a street corner, two housewives were muttering something while looking their way. In this day and age, merely walking with a little girl raised eyebrows. If there weren't people around, Shinichi would have walked Mai home, but he decided to split and head back to his own apartment.

"Mai, I'll give you this."

Shinichi pulled out the doll he'd won at the crane game out of his pocket.

"Are you sure?" Mai asked, tempted.

"It's a reward. Because you're being so good by helping around your house."

"Thank you, Haruna's big brother."

Mai put on a smile as she took it.

After seeing off her receding figure, Shinichi walked home to his apartment.

When he opened the sliding door, a scream rang out.

Haruna was in the middle of changing in the Japanese-style

room they used as a bedroom.

"Shin, at least knock!"

She looked furious as she threw a stuffed animal at him.

"You're so dramatic."

Without heeding her, Shinichi took off his jacket and put it on a hanger.

"I'm a woman, so treat me with proper delicacy," she said cheekily.

Until just the other day, she'd been running around the room naked and pestering him to take a bath with her. Recently, though, she seemed overly sensitive to his gaze. Was it what they called the onset of puberty?

He took a beer out of the fridge and went to the other room, which had the low table and TV.

The three of them—Naoko, Haruna, and Shinichi—lived in this old two-room apartment that had been built nearly thirty years ago. It was by no means easy living, but to Shinichi, the peace and quiet were irreplaceable.

He heard the sound of sirens in the distance.

"I wonder if there was a fire somewhere," Haruna came and asked.

"No, that's not a fire truck. It's a police car," he replied from bitter memory.

As the sound of the siren came closer, he became uneasy. The neighborhood was on the lonely side, and apparently, molestation cases weren't rare.

He became worried and emailed Naoko on his phone. The immediate reply was that she had overtime and would be a little late.

As he watched Naoko's back while she cleaned up after dinner in the kitchen, Shinichi looked for a chance to start his conversation. Haruna was in the bath by herself.

"Hey, sis," he called to Naoko, and she turned around. "I quit my job today. This month, I might not be able to bring that much money home, but I will next month, all right?"

He'd tried his best to make it sound like nothing, but Naoko looked at him with surprise. "Why? You liked that place so much."

Her expression gradually clouded. Maybe she was going over why he might have quit.

"There was a guy I didn't like and I got in a fight."

He couldn't bring himself to tell her he'd been dismissed.

Since he'd left reform school nine years ago, he'd been meaning to work hard but changed jobs time and again for the same old reason. On every such occasion he felt like cursing his black record, but he could never gripe about it to Naoko.

"I'll start looking again tomorrow, so yeah."

"Do you want me to ask at work?" Naoko worked at a flower shop near Ikebukuro station.

"No..." If they found out about his record, Naoko might suffer too—but he swallowed those words. "Early mornings aren't for me."

Beyond that, neither of them managed to get out a word. As though to break the heavy silence, the doorbell rang.

With some relief, Shinichi turned his eyes to the door.

"Coming." His sister went and opened it with the chain still in place.

"Excuse us for bothering you at such a late hour. We're police..."

At the word, Naoko's shoulders twitched, and her eyes turned to Shinichi.

He didn't recall doing anything at all to warrant this visit. Even so, his heart shriveled and ached. When Naoko removed the chain and opened the door all the way, he saw two men in suits standing there.

"There was an incident nearby, so we'd like to ask a few things," one of the men said.

Feeling intense palpitations, Shinichi stood up and headed to Naoko's side.

The man continued, "Are you acquainted with the Yokoses who live nearby?"

"Yokose… You mean the landlord of these apartments?" replied Naoko.

The detective who was doing the talking was well-built and imposing. Yet the tall one behind him was the one whose sight sent an intense shock through Shinichi.

For a moment, he doubted his eyes, but when they met the man's as he glanced back, Shinichi felt certain.

Nobuhito Natsume—somehow he remembered the name.

Why was he here? It was beyond confusing.

It seemed Natsume had also recognized Shinichi, and relaxing his expression somewhat, he greeted Shinichi with just his eyes.

"A resident who got home called to report that there was a dead body at the Yokoses'…"

"Did Mai make the report?" Naoko asked with a pained expression.

"Yes. The deceased is her father, Toru Yokose."

"And how is Mai…" Naoko barely managed.

"Currently, she is in police custody. But having found her father in such a state, she seems too shocked to answer—"

"Why in the world…" Shinichi interrupted without thinking.

"It appears that he was murdered with a solid blow to his head."

Murdered—Shinichi gulped when he heard the word.

"At this time, given the condition of the room, we believe that it was a burglary. We have eyewitness reports of Mr. Yokose getting home around six… Did you see any suspicious persons in the vicinity around that time?"

"I was working past seven and only came home a little before eight."

"Where are you employed?" the detective asked Naoko, and she gave them the flower shop's name and address. Natsume, hanging behind, jotted them down.

"I saw Mai there just before she got home," Shinichi mumbled.

"Wha-" Naoko looked at him. "You did?"

"Yeah…"

"What time was that?" the detective asked.

"I think around six twenty."

After receiving the doll from Shinichi, Mai had gone home smiling. Immediately after that, she'd found her dad murdered. It hurt him to imagine her shock.

"Did you happen to see any suspicious persons at that time?"

"Not really… Just two housewives standing around and talking."

"By the way, where were you before that?"

The detective's eyes seemed to sharpen. An alibi?

Natsume took one step forward and opened his mouth for the first time. "Please don't be offended. As far as that goes, we ask everyone we talk to."

Shinichi candidly shared his actions before and after six o'clock: loitering near Otsuka station, playing the arcade crane game before heading home.

The detectives listened in silence, but Shinichi felt more and more anxious even as he spoke.

He realized he didn't have a decisive alibi. He hadn't dropped by a store. He hadn't run into an acquaintance. As for the arcade, he'd only played the crane game outside. There hadn't been any spectators, either.

Naoko was looking at Shinichi with worry.

"Is there anyone who can testify about that for you?"

Shinichi could only lower his eyes at the detective's question.

As he did, he caught a glimpse of Naoko's hands. They were trembling slightly.

Perhaps she, too, feared that the detectives might zero in on Shinichi.

Even after getting into bed, he couldn't begin to calm down.

Next to him, he could hear Haruna breathing softly, asleep.

"Sis, you awake?" Shinichi murmured, looking up at the dim ceiling.

"Yeah."

"I…knew one of those detectives."

"Huh?" Naoko sounded surprised.

"He's a judiciary technical officer called Natsume who handled my case at juvie."

"Why would someone from…"

"I'm not sure. Why would that man—"

"It's okay, Shin… You have nothing to worry about," Naoko said, sensing Shinichi's anxiety.

But the more he recalled Natsume's relentless gaze, which tried to wade into your heart, the less calm he felt.

Eleven years ago, Shinichi had been arrested for murdering his uncle. It was when he was fifteen. After the police interrogation, he was placed in a juvenile detention center. Natsume, who was charged with him, asked about his family environment, personal relationships, and mindset leading up to the crime in minute detail.

Unlike the interrogation by the police, Natsume's attitude throughout the interviews was gentle. With a warm, enveloping gaze, he listened to Shinichi talk about his background. Natsume was a type of adult that Shinichi hadn't met before.

But he only felt creeped out by the man's warmth. It could all be a trick to peek into his heart. Shinichi absolutely couldn't let his guard down, not against this man, and stuck to ambiguous replies, stubbornly refusing to show his true self during the interviews.

All he ever said face to face with Natsume was that adults were repulsive; that he hadn't come across a decent grownup; that the only one he could look up to was his sister, who was three years older than him.

Shinichi didn't remember much about his parents, who passed away in a traffic accident when he was five. He and Naoko had been taken in by their only relative, Yuya Kimura, their mother's younger brother.

But this Kimura was scum.

A single man, he was gainfully employed, but it seemed he showed completely different faces to the outside world and in the house. If he didn't like anything, he didn't hesitate to raise his hand at Shinichi and Naoko and to allow only the barest of meals, during which he'd place the plate on the floor and not let them eat until they obediently pretended to be dogs. Through intense violence, and by completely shattering their self-esteem, Kimura dominated their young minds and bodies. That abuse continued for ten years.

Although Naoko was doing well as a student, she gave up on high school and started working at a hamburger shop. With that salary, she provided for Shinichi, buying meals for his growing appetite and whatever else he needed. Their wan wish then was to run away in a few years.

When Shinichi was fifteen, Naoko confided to him that a certain man had proposed to her. She'd been dating him without telling Kimura. A full-time employee at the burger shop, Isobe seemed to be sincere about Naoko, and even wanted Shinichi to come live with them until he graduated from high school once they got married.

But when Kimura found out, he attempted to mess everything up. It was then that Shinichi realized his uncle's true wickedness.

Shinichi didn't think the action he took was a mistake.

Murder was bad. He knew that. But he didn't think killing someone was the worst thing a person could do. More insidious and wicked people existed in the world.

After he turned himself in to the police, Shinichi couldn't stop worrying about Naoko. He thought Isobe might leave her because her younger brother had been arrested. Yet, Naoko and Isobe got married, and while Shinichi was in reform school, Haruna was born.

Shinichi meant to set out on his own after leaving the reformatory. He wanted Naoko to be happy.

But by the time he did, Naoko had broken up with Isobe and was living alone with Haruna. She wouldn't tell him why, either.

Was it the stigma of a murderer pinned on him, or were the deep scars she'd received at Kimura's hands the distant cause—

On the morning of the next day, with a job search magazine in hand, Shinichi made many calls. He contacted around twenty companies, but as expected, most of them demurred. Even so, one promised him an interview.

Shinichi hurriedly wrote his resume, got dressed, and headed to the food manufacturer located in Komagome.

He was rejected. When they asked him what he'd done after graduating from middle school, the endpoint of his educational history, for the first time Shinichi told them the truth. Even if he managed to be hired, he was sick and tired of being let go when they inevitably learned about his past. Maybe some people were ready to judge him by who he was now.

But that fleeting hope was quickly dashed. Chewing over his

disappointment, he got off the train at Otsuka station.

When he came to the crane game outside the station-front arcade, he stopped.

It was a day with no yields, but he could bring Haruna a gift at least. That morning, Naoko had told her about the case at Mai's, and it had wrecked Haruna.

Inserting a hundred-yen coin, he hit the button with perfect timing and netted a Momo-chan doll just like the day before.

"Bravo."

Shinichi turned around in surprise at the voice. Natsume was watching him with a smile on his face.

"Wow, in one try. I wanted that doll too and tried several times, but forget it."

The transparent excuse rubbed Shinichi the wrong way. Natsume must have been tailing him or checking his alibi.

"Coach me, will you?"

Natsume pulled some coins out of his wallet and started playing. No matter how many times he tried, the doll slipped off the crane. Unperturbed, he kept playing again and again.

"This is the one you gave Mai yesterday, right? Momo-chan. So you played here," asked Natsume, staring at the dolls in the case.

Really? A man your age saying "Momo-chan" like that? Shinichi spat inside, but said, "Yeah, I did."

"Yesterday, while we were questioning her, Mai was hugging hers the entire time."

Picturing the scene tore Shinichi up. He slapped Natsume's hand, which was over the button, hard the next instant. The crane descended and grabbed a doll.

"Wow!" cried Natsume, just about springing for joy as the doll fell into the chute.

"What're you gonna do with it?" Shinichi pointed out coldly.

"I'm giving it to my daughter."

Natsume held the doll with a happy smile.

Come to think of it, at the juvenile detention center, Natsume had talked about his family just once. Shinichi seemed to recall a daughter who'd been three or four at the time, which meant she was in middle school by now.

"Middle schoolers these days wouldn't want one, you know," warned Shinichi.

"I'm sure, in most cases. But my daughter's been lying on a hospital bed for nearly ten years now. I wanted to put one by her pillow."

Shinichi thought he saw the fond face of a father peeking through Natsume's faint smile. "Is she sick or something?"

Natsume didn't answer the question. "Would you like to get some coffee nearby, as my way of saying thank you?"

"An interrogation, huh?" Shinichi responded with sarcasm.

"No. A genuine thank you."

Putting the doll in his bag, Natsume began walking. Shinichi followed after him, not seeing much of a choice.

The doubt Shinichi had from the night before grew as he watched the man's back.

Why was he here? Most judiciary technical officers were qualified clinical therapists, pros in the field of psychology. When they'd first met, Natsume looked to be in his late twenties. That man was walking in front of him now as a detective.

Had he gotten fed up with having to face bad apples and changed jobs? No, entering the police force meant confronting greater evil.

As Shinichi wondered, the man's slim back began to look ominous and intimidating.

"It seems that you quit your job yesterday," Natsume said after taking a sip of coffee.

Shinichi mentally clicked his tongue as he faced the man.

Of course Natsume—that's to say, the police, had been duly investigating him. How was this a genuine thank you? Apart from using a cafe rather than a gloomy interrogation room, they were grilling him all right.

"Have you decided on your next job," Natsume asked.

"I'm looking right now. And you, detective work seems to leave you with plenty of spare time. A murder close by, and you play at an arcade and chat at a coffee shop."

"On duty at that. You see, I was able to confirm a few things."

"That a 'person of interest' is sitting in front of you, for one? Investigations can't be too hard when someone who has killed lives right nearby, yeah? It's always like this. I try to live honestly, but my record gets in the way. Everyone looks at me through a tinted lens."

In response to Shinichi's bluntness, Natsume patiently gazed into his eyes. Shinichi hated that look.

"Come on," the detective said, "not everyone in the world looks at you weird."

"Dunno about that," Shinichi threw out. "The fact is, whenever there's a case, police flock to me. It's true that I quit my job yesterday. You probably looked into it already, so hell, I didn't quit, I was dismissed. For no reason. Just like you saw and felt, we don't have extra money lying around. I bet you can come up with a storyline where I wanted money and snuck into the Yokoses' as a burglar."

"I'm sorry, but that's not the storyline I'm thinking of," Natsume said, his chin on his hand, pensive.

"What do you mean?"

"There's zero evidence that anything of monetary value was stolen from Mr. Yokose's residence. The perp seems to have gone through the living-room cabinet and closets, but the wallet in Mr. Yokose's pants was left behind, and no bankbooks or cards seem to be missing. True, maybe there was some expensive item that neither we nor Mai are aware of."

"Weren't there fingerprints or something?"

"Nope."

Shinichi was disappointed. If there were any fingerprints he'd be in the clear.

"Mr. Yokose must have come home when the burglar was going through the living room. Looks like the perp found a nearby video camera and lay in wait by the door. Striking Mr. Yokose's head with it as soon as he entered, the perp then took off. Mr. Yokose was found collapsed by the door, with a bloodstained video camera close by. It wasn't your usual small one for families, but a heftier model for pros."

Shinichi recalled Haruna saying that Mai's had a large television and an expensive-looking video camera.

"Are you allowed to blabber to someone like me about this?"

"You're right." Natsume grinned wryly. "Keep this conversation between us."

Natsume discussing operational secrets so readily almost made Shinichi worry about the safety of his neighborhood. The man was fairly unimpressive as a detective.

"When did you change jobs?" Shinichi tried asking.

"I quit being a judiciary technical officer ten years ago, and when I was thirty, I took the police employment exam. After graduating from the academy I served at police boxes for nearly six years, but recently, I transferred to my current section."

Why had Natsume gone as far as to abandon his juvie job to join the police force? Even Shinichi could imagine that taking up an entirely different line of work at thirty posed considerable difficulties.

"Why did you become a cop?"

"I wonder… Maybe it was those police dramas."

Shinichi immediately recognized that as an evasion.

"If I could give one reason, I must have wanted to do it for my family."

"But you don't seem cut out for it," Shinichi told him.

"That might be true..." Natsume stood up, bill in hand. "But cut out for it or not, you hurry and find a job too. In order to live, and to protect your dear ones, you need to work."

With that, Natsume left the coffee shop.

"Haruna, clean up your own messes!"

Shinichi could hear Naoko's reproach from the other room. Usually it ended with this one shout, but today she went on to lecture her daughter at length. In time, he heard Haruna blubbering.

He put his can of beer down on the table and went to check the situation in the other room.

Haruna's eyes were red from blubbering. Naoko was bending down to catch her gaze as she lectured her.

"Sis, could you leave it at that."

"You stay out of it!" Naoko shot back.

Shinichi, who'd never seen her look so severe, backed down.

"Hey, Haruna..." Naoko admonished in a calmer tone. "You're big now so you have to start being able to do things for yourself. You can't just rely on others all the time. Do you understand?"

Haruna nodded, wiping her tears with her hands. "I'm sorry..." she apologized, looking at Naoko.

"Good girl," Naoko stroked her daughter's head. "I'll brush your hair. Over here."

Naoko went to the vanity and placed Haruna on her knee. As she gently combed Haruna's hair, the girl's expression rapidly turned into a smile.

Watching the scene, Shinichi couldn't but admire what a great big sister Naoko was.

Neither of them knew much about the love of a parent. After

they lost both and were adopted by Kimura, their days were filled with abuse. It was often said that people who faced abuse as kids repeated the cycle with their own kids; that was probably because they didn't know an adult's love and had no idea how to show it to their own children. But Naoko, who'd been thoroughly abused by Kimura, showered Haruna with love. She raised her daughter as though her life depended on it. She was an amazing person.

How about himself? If he were to start his own family, would he be able to treasure it like Naoko?

Shinichi had never been in love. Or rather, he always gave up on love. Even if he did come to like and date someone, how she might respond to his past when she found out scared him. And if he ended up marrying a woman he loved and had kids, he didn't know whether he'd be able to shower them with love, and that scared him.

To protect your dear ones—

He recalled what Natsume had said to him at the coffee shop.

Was he ever going to meet someone that dear to him? Would he ever start a family he'd protect no matter what?

On the next day too, Shinichi made calls throughout the morning, job magazine in hand. Every time he was turned down, he crossed out the wanted with a red pen. By lunch, the pages were very red. Even so, he was able to schedule interviews with two firms. One was a restaurant in Shinjuku, and the other was a construction-related business in Nippori. He was heading out to Shinjuku where the restaurant was; his visit to the company in Nippori was arranged for the next day.

The restaurant interview, as expected, did not go well. This time too, when he honestly told them about his reformatory past, they chose their words carefully to avoid incurring a grudge, and rejected him.

It was understandable. But he couldn't give up. The other

company interviewing him tomorrow might hire him, he kept on encouraging himself on his train ride home.

By the time he got off at Otsuka station, however, he was feeling as worthless as a pebble.

When he glanced toward the gaming arcade by the station, his legs froze. Natsume was playing a crane game at the store-front.

The man had taken on the machine next to the one he'd tried the day before. Absorbed, he was glaring at the case's contents.

Shinichi decided to move along so Natsume wouldn't notice, but as he passed by the man's back, the crane's movement caught his attention, and he looked. The arms picked up a doll and dropped it in the chute. At that moment, Natsume cheered and leapt for joy.

The man turned Shinichi's way, and their eyes met.

"O-Oh. Hello," Natsume said with an embarrassed laugh.

"What sort of grownup…" Shinichi muttered, and almost laughed too.

"I'm ashamed." In Natsume's hand was a different doll from the day before, a bear.

"Did your daughter like the Momo-chan you won yesterday?" Shinichi asked.

"When I put it at her bedside, her eyes responded a bit. Well, I thought they did. So I wanted to get more kinds."

Natsume smiled. Shinichi thought it was a smile that betrayed loneliness.

"Is your daughter's condition that bad?"

"A head injury left her in a vegetative state. Although as her family, I don't like her being called a vegetable. My daughter is my daughter."

Maybe that had something to do with Natsume becoming a police officer, because his gaze, which had been calm, seemed to take on fire for a moment. But Shinichi chose not to dig deeper.

"Great timing. I had something I wanted to ask a local resident such as yourself. Walk with me for a bit," Natsume said and sauntered ahead.

"Like what?" Shinichi asked, following him.

"Were you close to Mai?"

"Not really. She's my niece Haruna's classmate, so when I see her I at least say hi."

"Interacting with Mai, did you notice something?"

"Nah…just that she's quiet or maybe a little gloomy for a kid. Why?"

"Apparently, there'd been anonymous calls to child services from several months ago that Mai was being abused by her father."

"Abused?" The word cast a dark shadow across Shinichi's heart.

"It wasn't just one or two calls, but frequent. Each time, a staff member from child services met and talked to her father, but he adamantly claimed that there was no such fact and chased them off."

"Are you saying it has a bearing on the case?"

"No, I'm not sure. But looking into things that might not falls on us the police, too."

"Why not just ask Mai?"

"She isn't talking. Maybe the shock of seeing her father dead was too intense, but she won't talk to us no matter what we ask her," Natsume said, looking straight into Shinichi's eyes.

"Mr. Koide, it says here you graduated from middle school in 2000, but what have you been doing from then until now?" a man in overalls who'd introduced himself as the chief asked, his eyes on Shinichi's resume.

Shinichi, sitting across the man for the interview, clenched his fists. When the chief stared at him, he felt an urge to look away, and his head began to bow. His gaze fixed on a spot on the desktop right in front of him.

"Were you what they call a 'freeter'? No set occupation, as a lifestyle choice?" the chief asked.

Shinichi made up his mind and looked into the chief's eyes. "When I was in my third year of middle school, I killed someone and spent two years in a reformatory…"

He went on to lay bare his personal history. That he'd finished middle school while so detained. That after leaving the reformatory, he'd worked many jobs but never for long. That he had a sister and a niece who were his dear family and wanted more than anything to work. That he hoped to acquire specialized skills that would keep him employed.

The chief spent some time alternating between looking at Shinichi's face and his resume. "Are you healthy?" he asked.

"Yes…"

"We do very hard labor. Early mornings good with you?"

"Yes, I am fine with them," Shinichi answered.

"Then could you come by at seven the day after tomorrow?"

"Mom, what's going on?" Haruna said, surprised at the dishes lining the dining table.

No wonder—compared to their usual fare, this parade was mindbogglingly luxurious.

After the interview today, Shinichi had emailed Naoko that he'd landed a job. Immediately, he'd gotten a call from her.

Congratulations—she'd sounded like she was crying.

As they surrounded the table as a family, Haruna said with her cheeks stuffed with sushi, "It'd be nice if every day could be like this."

"Today is special," Naoko nipped it in the bud, laughing.

"It seems to be tough work, but the salary isn't bad. So maybe not every day, but we could have a meal like this once a month,"

Shinichi declared with some pride.

"Thank you," Naoko and Haruna politely bowed, then spurt out giggling.

The doorbell rang.

"Coming!" Naoko called out and made to stand up, but Shinichi said, "I'll go," and headed to the front door and opened it.

When he saw Natsume standing outside in the hallway, a sigh escaped him.

He didn't want to see this man's face now. For once, they were sitting together happily, and he felt aggrieved that the mood was being spoiled.

"What do you want?" he lashed out.

"I apologize about the late hour. I was hoping to speak to your older sister and Haruna a bit."

"Concerning?"

Hearing Natsume's words, Naoko came to the front door with Haruna.

"It's about Mai…" Crouching there at the front door, Natsume looked into Haruna's eyes. "Listen, Haruna… Did Mai ever tell you anything about her father?"

Perhaps feeling nervous in face of a stranger, the girl remained silent.

"For instance, that she was picked on by him?"

Haruna looked up to Naoko.

"Haruna, did you hear about anything like that from Mai?"

The girl shook her head in response to her mother's question and said, "Nope, nothing."

"How about you, ma'am, did Mai ever share anything of the sort?"

"Nothing that comes to mind…" Naoko replied, sounding worried. "Why do you ask?"

"It seems Mai had been abused by her father. There had been

anonymous accusations phoned in to child services, so I thought you might have heard about it from Haruna and made the reports…"

"It wasn't me. Why did you think it was me?"

"You spoke to Mai fairly often at the park according to one of your neighbors."

"She's Haruna's friend, so I do when I see her, but I didn't notice anything like that."

"You mentioned that you work, ma'am, but on a few occasions you were seen with her on weekday afternoons."

"Yes. My shop does bike deliveries, so I often pass by here, too."

"I see. Sorry for disturbing you so late." Natsume looked at Shinichi. "Did you decide on a job, Shinichi?" he asked.

Shinichi nodded glumly.

"Ah. Good luck. Well, if you happen to notice anything, please contact me." With a light bow, Natsume started to leave.

"Excuse me," Naoko called out. "How is Mai?"

"She's in the protection of child services."

"I see…"

With Natsume gone they returned to the dining table, but all three of them had lost their appetites for the rare feast.

"Shin, is there anyone you like?" Naoko asked abruptly while he was in bed staring at the dim ceiling.

"Wh-Why, that's…sudden."

It was the first time Naoko had addressed the issue, so Shinichi was flustered.

"No reason. I just wanted to ask."

"Unfortunately, no. I'm not interested anyway."

It was a lie. He couldn't tell her that he was afraid of loving someone because of his record.

"I'll think about it if you find someone good for you, sis."

"Thanks, but I'm okay…as long as I have Haruna," Naoko said, a hint of loneliness creeping into her voice.

Was her truncated married life with Isobe making her say that? Why had she broken up with him anyway?

"Hey, sis… Why did you break up with Isobe? Don't tell me it was because of that case…" Shinichi made bold and asked what he hadn't been able to until now.

"It wasn't related. He just wasn't the type who could love a child with all his heart. Until we married he was nice, but after Haruna was born, he changed. He used to hit her and call it discipline… That's why…"

So something like that had happened.

"I have Haruna. I'm happy with that. That's why I want you to hurry and find your own happiness."

Shinichi turned his eyes to Haruna, who was sleeping next to him.

"Oh, I'm happy," he said. He was more than happy with just Naoko and Haruna.

The three of them, getting along and living together—that was Shinichi's one and only wish and happiness. He believed that the time to relinquish that happiness was when Haruna had a new father.

"I'll be her father," Shinichi muttered.

"Thanks…"

Hearing Naoko's tearful voice, Shinichi closed his eyes.

He woke to Haruna's crying.

When he looked next to him, she and Naoko weren't there. Haruna seemed to be blubbering behind the sliding door.

The clock said it was still before six.

What was it, so early in the morning? Was Naoko scolding her again?

Rubbing his drowsy eyes, Shinichi got up. When he slid open

the door, he found Haruna crying with her head on the table.

"What's the matter? Did you get in trouble with sis again?"

He looked around the kitchen, but there was no sign of Naoko.

"Mom is… Mom is…"

Haruna was still crying as he handed him a piece of paper. Shinichi, bewildered, followed the writing on it.

"To Haruna. Mom needs to go to someplace far away for a while. Listen well to what Shin says and be a good girl. Your Mom."

"What the…" Shinichi had no idea what the note meant.

"Was it my fault? Was it because I said something weird that mom left?"

"Weird? What did you say to sis?" Shinichi asked. When Haruna didn't reply, he pressed, "Haruna—this is important. Tell me exactly what you said to sis."

"Last week…on the way home from cram school, Mai told me that her dad was videoing her these days… He'd take off her clothes and get her naked and touch her all over and she didn't like it, but if she did it, he got in a good mood and stopped hitting her and gave her yummy food and bought her any toy she wanted… So she was letting him."

Listening to Haruna, Shinichi's chest had tightened. Rage simmered up from deep inside him, but he asked in as calm a tone as he could, "And you told sis?"

"Yeah. Then mom said I couldn't tell anyone."

Shinichi felt certain.

It was Naoko who'd murdered Yokose. No, rather than murder—she must have ended up accidentally killing him. If she'd meant to kill him, she'd have brought along a knife or some other weapon.

Through talking to Mai, Naoko must have caught on to Yokose's abuse a while ago, from the traces, the bruises and scars that most people would miss.

The anonymous caller who'd continued to contact child services was probably also Naoko. But they never even got close to solving the problem. Then Haruna told her all that.

She must have ransacked the Yokoses' living room to steal a DVD or some other recording of Mai naked. She probably intended to hand the decisive evidence to child services or the police. But while she was going through the room, Yokose came home—

Tears welled up in Shinichi's eyes.

At the same time, that repulsive memory revived in him.

One winter day, when he was in the third year of middle school—he started to feel ill, left early, and came home to Kimura's condominium.

When he entered through the front door, he heard a woman crying in the room Kimura used as his bedroom. When Shinichi knocked, it was Naoko's voice that said, "Don't come in!"

Worried, he ignored her and opened the door.

It was when he witnessed the scene that he understood for the first time. Kimura was naked and stretched out on top of the bed. Next to him, Naoko gathered her clothes, which had been practically torn off her, to hide her bare skin. Nearby were a camera and scattered toys to make a plaything of her body—

Where was she now?

Driven by unease, Shinichi tried calling and emailing Naoko's phone, but there was no response.

"Hey, Haruna…" he said, to which the blubbering girl raised her face, "you want your mom to come home, right?"

Wiping her tears away with her hands, his niece nodded vigorously.

Right. Haruna needs Naoko.

"Then work with me."

Shinichi asked her about the times she went to play at Mai's house and made her recall, in as much detail as possible, the house's floor plan and furniture. In addition, he looked at the papers from the last few days and pounded into his head the articles on the Yokose residence case.

Until just the day before, he'd felt bitter about not having a complete alibi; now he was thankful.

They were good. He'd be able to save Naoko. The police just wanted to arrest any culprit. He was ready to put his life on the line once more to protect Naoko.

"—That day, I'd gotten fired from my job and didn't care anymore."

Natsume, seated across the table, fixed Shinichi with his gaze. "So...you entered Mr. Yokose's home to burglarize it?"

"Yeah, that's right...because Yokose's place seemed like it'd have a lot of money. I broke the rear window and was going through the living room, but that guy immediately came home. So we startled to wrestle, and I hit him in the head with a nearby video camera. Since I was upset, I forgot to steal the money and just fled. There were women standing around and talking near the house, so I tried taking the long way back to the apartment, but boom, I ran into Mai."

One hour after turning himself in to the precinct station, Shinichi faced Natsume in an interrogation room.

He was basing his testimony on what the papers had reported and on Haruna's recollections. He winged the parts he wasn't sure about, saying he'd been too upset to remember well.

Once Shinichi finished going over his story, Natsume let out a small sigh. Then, the detective slowly shook his head.

"Unfortunately, you couldn't have killed Mr. Yokose."

"What do you mean?" Shinichi asked.

"That day, neighbors witnessed you and Mai near her house at six twenty. They're fairly certain about the time. From where you met Mai, it's at least a five-minute walk for a child. You said you played the crane game at six. That's only fifteen minutes—it doesn't make sense psychologically for a culprit to murder someone, immediately go play a crane game, and hurry back close to the scene. It's impossible, realistically speaking."

"Detective Natsume, you're an incredibly honest person, aren't you," laughed Shinichi. "My playing the crane game at the arcade at six is a lie. I had on me a doll that I'd won earlier."

"At what time?"

"I wonder, let's see," Shinichi said, tugging in his memories of that day. It was shortly after three, he believed, that he'd shot out of the pub after being dismissed by the manager. Then he'd wandered on foot from Ikebukuro to Otsuka. "I think it must've been a little past four."

"For the gaming arcade by Otsuka station?"

"Yup. Then I wandered around near the station for a while and came up with burglarizing Yokose's place."

When Shinichi gave this reply, he felt like Natsume's eyes took on a different cast.

What was he thinking?

Maybe he'd hoped Shinichi would get back on his feet. Maybe the man felt betrayed and disappointed. No, that wasn't it—

The moment Shinichi realized that the gaze reflected pity, Natsume opened his mouth. "That doll you gave Mai wasn't there then."

All Shinichi could say was: "Wh-What do you mean…"

"That day, an employee whose shift was ending at six changed the prizes to new ones to finish up—completing the task just a minute or two before six, according to the employee's testimony. In other words, you won that doll right afterwards. To confirm your alibi, we even looked into the fingerprints on the doll. Mai's had that employee's fingerprints."

On duty at that. You see, I was able to confirm a few things.

So that was what Natsume had been looking into. He hadn't just been goofing off.

Dammit—Shinichi gritted his teeth in frustration.

With a knock, a man came into the interrogation room. He whispered something to Natsume.

"You can just go home or stick around for a while," Natsume offered, standing up. He exited the room, leaving behind the detective who'd been taking it all down.

Shinichi hung his head, defeated.

After nearly an hour, Natsume returned to the room and sat down across the table.

"My sister, huh?" Shinichi had gathered that much.

"That's right. I was pretty sure she'd turn herself in. But before doing so, she apparently wanted more than anything to go to child services. More than anything, she wanted to give Mai a hug. And to apologize to her."

"Why would…my sister…"

"She wanted evidence that Mai was being sexually abused by Mr. Yokose and snuck into their house."

Going through the living room, she found a DVD that seemed like what she was looking for, and that was when someone came home, according to Naoko. From how the voice called for Mai at the front door, she immediately knew that it was Yokose. Afraid that with only a woman's strength she'd quickly be subdued, she took the video camera in hand and watched by the door. Although she was hoping to slip past, Yokose came into the living room, so she hit his head with the camera and ran away.

"She said she just had to bring home evidence of Mai's abuse…and all she could think of was not getting caught then and there. She hadn't planned on killing him, but…she did harbor hatred for Mr. Yokose and wouldn't deny murderous intent. Her own words."

"Since when did you suspect her?" Shinichi said, glaring at

Natsume.

"When I first visited you, my colleague announced that there was a dead body at the Yokose residence, and your sister immediately asked if Mai had made the call. As though there were no chance that the deceased was Mai—that's when I had my initial doubts. I wondered if maybe she'd heard from you about meeting Mai on the way, but that wasn't the case. What's more, when people you know die, the first thing you normally ask is how it happened. But your sister was only interested in Mai."

At that moment, Mai's shock upon coming home to her father's corpse must have been all Naoko could think of. It had been her undoing.

"Idiot..." Shinichi muttered, and the tears came when he did.

It was somebody else's problem. Why should Naoko and her girl become unhappy to save others? No one ever helped them when they were being abused.

He wrung out the words that had been lying in his heart. "He was a scumbag who'd do that to a little kid who couldn't fight back, to his own kid. Why should sis be punished for someone like him?"

"You can't kill a person, no matter what. You can't hurt someone," Natsume told him quietly.

"I...I wanted to trade places with her. Sis is an amazing person."

"Your sister said she couldn't let you suffer a second time."

Shinichi lifted his head.

Had Naoko talked about that, too?

One winter day, when he was in the third year of middle school—it was when he opened Kimura's bedroom door that Shinichi understood for the first time.

Kimura was naked and stretched out on top of the bed. A knife was sticking out his back. Next to him, Naoko gathered her clothes, which had been practically torn off her, to hide her bare skin. On top of the bloodstained bed were a camera and scattered toys to make a plaything of her body—

Apparently, Kimura had blackmailed her into breaking up with Isobe upon finding out about their relationship. He'd threatened to show her lover all the footage of her being shamed ever since she was a child. Naoko cried and told Shinichi that she'd meant to kill herself after Kimura.

How long had Kimura been doing this to Naoko? How much had she endured to protect her helpless little brother?

Shinichi frantically stopped Naoko when she said she intended to confess to the police.

As an eighteen year old, Naoko would likely be punished severely for committing murder, even if juvenile law were applied to her. They knew that the death penalty was a possibility once you were eighteen. Shinichi, who was fifteen, wouldn't be punished as harshly.

More than that, he didn't want Naoko to give up Isobe and her chance at happiness that had arrived at long last. Given what she'd suffered until now, she absolutely needed to become happy.

Shinichi resolved to take her place and, mustering all his will, convinced her.

He didn't think his course of action then was mistaken.

"I failed you when I didn't catch on during our interviews at the juvenile detention center."

"You didn't fail…" Shinichi rejected Natsume's mea culpa.

Indeed, thanks to that, Haruna was here.

"Please take care of Haruna—that's her message for you. From now on, protect your dear ones in a different way," Natsume urged with an impassioned look.

I know… I know…

Shinichi was going to be in the same position as Kimura. He

would never become that sort of grownup, though. He would never let Haruna go through what they'd had to.

And together with Haruna, he'd await Naoko's return.

"I know," Shinichi affirmed.

Heartless

"The next stop is Takada-no-Baba, Takada-no-Baba..."

As the announcement ran, a man who'd been reading a comic magazine and looked to be an office worker stood up.

Masayuki Matsushita slowly approached the man's seat. Just as he thought, before leaving the train he'd left the magazine on the overhead rack. In a heartbeat, the magazine was Masayuki's. It was a popular one that had come out that day. He casually stuffed it into his bag and got off the train.

Most of the people on the platform looked tired. Today was a Monday. Having thoroughly enjoyed their weekends, they were facing the start of the workweek with dread.

Masayuki had been the same as a company man. On days after outings with his wife and son, he'd stood on the platform with the same look, no doubt.

Remembering a bit of his past made his mood sink.

He desperately drove off his pesky memories. Lots of popular magazines were sold on Mondays, and it was time to make a living.

Approaching a trash bin, Masayuki pulled a metal tool out of his bag. He'd made it from a bent wire hanger and used it to fish magazines out of bins with narrow openings.

Passersby were staring at Masayuki.

When he first resorted to this livelihood, he'd felt self-conscious about being seen even just walking around town, but now he felt nothing.

Masayuki made five more rounds on the Yamanote line and collected nearly one hundred magazines. He sold them at a used bookstore in Ikebukuro and made 2,700 yen. Today's earnings were decent.

From where the bookstore was at the west entrance, he passed through the arcade toward the east entrance. It was before six but already getting dark. Coming into December, the cold had intensified a notch. Masayuki stuffed his hands into the pockets of his down jacket and walked toward the lights of the Sunshine 60 skyscraper.

He stopped by a convenience store. He'd made a reasonable amount of money today and planned to make dinner more extravagant than usual. He put a fried chicken boxed meal and a rice ball in his basket. Then, remembering, he added some prepackaged egg porridge as well and headed to the register.

When he reached the park, a few youths were skateboarding in the main plaza. The sound of wheels hitting pavement grated on his ears, but he ignored it and continued on.

Past the plaza, there was a dense growth of trees. Several tents made of tarp stood side by side and bags crammed with empty cans sat here and there. This was Masayuki's current abode. Nearly ten homeless people lived here.

Kon walked over to Masayuki, who didn't know his real name. The man came to be called that because he was always wearing his best and only *kon*, or navy blue, suit. Until a few years ago he'd been a middle manager at a major bank, a fact that seemed to prop up his ego even now.

"Good evening. How did your interview go?" Masayuki greeted him.

Kon made his living collecting aluminum cans but hadn't given up on his social reinstatement. He'd said he was going to be interviewed today by a company that took cleaning contracts for buildings.

"No luck," Kon replied moodily. "Well, it's a small company that can't afford a decent salary, so I wasn't sure myself."

Though not a bad person, he was proud to a fault. After parting ways with Kon, Masayuki peeked into Naka's tent.

"Naka, I've brought provisions," Masayuki greeted, and the old man, who'd buried himself in his sleeping bag, turned toward the voice. He started coughing.

"Hey, thank you always," Naka thanked Masayuki in a hoarse voice.

"Your cold still hasn't gotten better? Seems like it's only getting worse…"

The man looked gaunt and old ever since they'd first met, but this past week his cheeks seemed even more sunken.

Naka had come here three months ago. It was just a month after Masayuki had started his life here, so Naka was the only one newer than him. He was probably around sixty years old. He'd always lived in Aomori, he said, but after being laid off ten years ago, he'd tumbled down into homelessness and ended up in Tokyo.

"Why don't you go to the hospital?" Masayuki advised.

"I don't have that kind of money…" Naka laughed, coughing.

Masayuki had grown fond of Naka, who was unfalteringly tranquil even though he'd been living this way for ten years.

"I'll heat up the egg porridge that I bought you."

Going into the tent, Masayuki filled the pot with water and heated it over the portable gas stove. He poured the warm egg porridge into a bowl and handed it to Naka.

"Thank you…"

The old man came out of his sleeping bag and sipped the egg porridge.

"May I eat here too?"

Masayuki pulled his fried chicken set out of the convenience store bag and had his dinner with Naka.

"Masaa! Masaa!"

Hearing someone calling for him outside, Masayuki flipped open the tarp entrance to look out.

Sho was shouting outside Masayuki's tent.

"I'm over here," he called, and Sho made his way toward him.

"What, you were here all along? I've got booze for you, come over to my place." Peeking into the back, he added, "I'll give you some too, ol' geezer, so come on over."

Masayuki exchanged glances with Naka.

Though Masayuki didn't really feel like drinking, turning Sho down could cause complications. The guy looked around the same age as him, but here Sho was something of a boss. Masayuki and Naka left the tent together and followed Sho.

Sho's shack was slightly set off from everyone else's homes. It was noticeably large among the group of tents and had iron pipe pillars and veneer panel coverings. Masayuki had been inside a number of times, and with accoutrements like a television set and a soft-looking mattress, it seemed pretty comfortable.

Sho was skilled at using people, whether it was acting as a middleman for the open-air bookshops selling magazines on the street or pointing the newly homeless to gigs and squeezing some of their earnings from them. For a homeless fellow, he was quite prosperous.

Opening the door of the shack, he ushered them in. When Masayuki entered, he found Kon sitting there uncomfortably.

Expensive-looking bottles of alcohol were lined up inside. Sho grabbed one of them and poured out four cups.

"It ain't cheap, so be grateful," Sho said sitting cross-legged.

Coughing now and then, Naka sipped the booze.

"Shouldn't you cut that with water?" Masayuki thought to ask him, but Naka laughed and said, "I'm fine. They say alcohol is the best home remedy."

"Macallan… I used to drink this almost every day. Like at a Ginza club," Kon murmured with feeling, his cup to his mouth.

"Right, you said you used to be a department head at a large company. And look at you now. Can't make any sense of the world," Sho sneered.

Kon's expression instantly clouded. It seemed that his proud heart had been wounded.

The air in the shack seemed to bristle.

"Sho, why have you kept living like this?" Masayuki changed the topic, eager to dispel the oppressive mood.

"Why do you ask?"

"I mean, couldn't someone like you who's so good at handling people easily find a normal job?" Masayuki said.

Sho laughed loudly. "Fuck normal jobs. Look at this pops." He pointed at Kon. "He was used like a rag, and for all his fawning bowing and getting to a halfway respectable position, he was told he was useless and got laid off. I'd feel like an idiot. You see, I used to ride at the head of my biker pals. It'd be an honest shame for me to serve anyone. I stay because I rule as long as I'm here. In a sense, this place is like heaven to me."

"Thank you for the drink!"

Kon slammed his cup on the ground and left.

Masayuki had spoken up to temper the mood but instead ended up horribly disturbing the hornet's nest.

Naka just stared at Sho and indifferently drank his whiskey.

Sho was certainly coarse, but he had even been the head of a motorcycle gang. No wonder he was good at forcing others to do his bidding, Masayuki thought.

He studied the scorpion tattoo etched into the back of Sho's hand as the guy gulped down whiskey.

"Masa, I'll show you a new way to make money, so come with me tomorrow," Sho said.

"Okay, understood."

"All right, then come to the plaza in the morning at nine."

Jostled awake by a whooshing roar, Masayuki flew out of his sleeping bag. He looked around in his dark tent. Across the tarp, a myriad of fireworks were flying around and explosions echoed all over.

What on earth had happened?

When Masayuki left the tent, a firework popped at his feet. The fire spread to dry wood, and he hastily put it out by stomping on it with his shoes. From the tents around him, people were also jumping out in bewilderment.

"Get lost, social trash!" Three youths were launching skyrocket fireworks toward the tents and laughing.

Masayuki glared at them and clucked his tongue.

Recently, a lot of people harassed the homeless. It wasn't too bad when they were just causing trouble, but the previous week, a tent had been set on fire in Shinjuku and a homeless person had died. The culprit was still at large.

"Bastards, you don't screw around with me!" Sho raged as he got out of his shack and headed towards the plaza.

Masayuki watched to see whether he needed help, but Sho was beating up the three youths in no time. The guy hadn't led a motorcycle gang for nothing.

The kids desperately begged for forgiveness, but Sho's rampage didn't stop. Even if they'd provoked the fight, this was going too far. If it went on and became a police matter, they'd all be in trouble.

Masayuki reluctantly headed toward Sho.

"Bastards, don't underestimate me! I wouldn't give a shit if I beat you bloody and killed you!" Hollering, Sho continued to kick the three as they groveled on the ground.

"Sho, shouldn't you leave it at that. It'd be trouble if the police came..." Masayuki interceded.

Sho turned towards him and then immediately looked down at the three collapsed youths. After thinking for a bit, he pulled the trio's wallets from their pants pockets. He just took the bills out and tossed the wallets.

"Fees for our trouble. If you tattle to the police, I'll kill you, got it? Unlike you bastards, I have nothing to lose."

Even as Sho threatened them, the crying youths picked up their wallets and left the park.

"They go through with this even though they're small fry. Right?" Sho grinned and sought approval, but Masayuki couldn't nod.

The next morning, Masayuki ate the rice ball he'd bought the day before and made his way out of his tent to the plaza.

Sitting on a bench, Masayuki lit up and waited for Sho, but the guy was taking forever. Was he still asleep?

Having smoked the cigarette to its base, Masayuki threw it into an ashtray and headed to Sho's shack.

He knocked on the door, but there was no reply. After knocking several times, he tried opening it.

Sho was sleeping with a futon over his head.

"Morning. It's nine thirty already."

Masayuki shook Sho's body from above the futon. No response. He shook even harder. Still no response. He slowly peeled the futon away, then screamed.

Sho was lying face down, his head bashed into a pulpy mess.

Ten minutes after Masayuki made a report to the emergency number, a uniformed police officer appeared on a bicycle. Then it was as though a beehive had been poked. Several police cars came to blockade the park and to question the homeless, including Masayuki, who were living in the park.

"Your name?" one of the detectives asked Kon, his tone

bordering on rude, and his face contorting, probably at the smell.

"They call me Kon," Kon answered sulkily.

"Your actual name, the real one! Also, you probably don't have an address, so give your permanent one."

"I haven't done anything wrong, so why do you need my name? It's etiquette to give your own before asking someone."

"If you can't tell me here, you can come to the station."

"This is a human rights violation!" resisted Kon, getting into an argument with the detective.

The people who lived here had various backstories. No doubt, some balked at revealing themselves to the police.

Masayuki was one of them. What if his wife, Saeko, had put out a missing persons search? But after thinking about it, he silently scoffed at himself. Not a chance. Saeko must have submitted the divorce papers and moved back with her parents a good while ago.

Naka, who was standing next to Masayuki, started coughing hard.

"Are you okay?" a tall man wearing a suit came and asked Naka. "I'm very sorry you have to be in the cold. We'll be done soon, so please rest over here."

The man supported Naka over to a bench. He patted Naka's back. This man also seemed to be a detective, but what a difference from the one who was talking to Kon.

"What might your name be?" the man smiled and asked Naka.

"It's Yasutaro Nakajima—but here they call me Naka."

"Then can I call you that as well? Naka, have you always lived in Tokyo?"

"No, Tokyo, I came to recently. I'm from Aomori."

"Ah ha. I'm from Aomori, too. Where in Aomori?"

"Hachinoe."

"That's close to where I used to live..."

Smiling amiably, the man asked for Naka's permanent address, last current address, and whether he'd seen anything odd in the vicinity the night before.

The man came to Masayuki next. "Good afternoon. May I talk to you?" he said, and asked the same things he'd asked Naka.

Masayuki replied honestly, both about himself and how he'd found Sho's body.

"By the way, Sho, who passed away… Would you know his real name? It seems that people here only knew him as Sho."

"Well, he was Sho to me, too. Didn't you find a license or something?"

"No. We're searching the shack he lived in, but we haven't found anything to link him to an identity."

"I see."

"By the way, did anything unusual happen in this area recently?" the man asked further.

"Now that you mention it…"

Something did come to mind—the night before, some youths had launched rocket fireworks at the tents and gotten beaten up by Sho. Had they assaulted him in retaliation? Masayuki told the man about this.

"Launching fireworks at tents is just terrible. Did you see their faces?"

Masayuki nodded.

"If you see them again, or if others try that, please contact me," the man said, handing Masayuki his card.

It said: *East Ikebukuro Precinct - Nobuhito Natsume.*

Although the blockades were lifted from the park the next day, most of the homeless who'd been living there gathered their belongings and left. Perhaps they felt that the place was unsafe and that the police coming back from time to time could be troublesome.

Masayuki also struggled over whether to leave. But he wa
reluctant to abandon Naka, who was ill and couldn't easily mov
Masayuki decided to stay with him.

After a few days, the police made themselves scarce as wel
With the exception of one man—

"Good afternoon."

Natsume came by while Masayuki was crushing aluminu
cans in front of his tent. Masayuki lightly nodded back and re
turned his focus on the cans.

"What are you doing?" asked Natsume, watching the proce
with open curiosity.

"I'm crushing them to sell them."

"How much do you make?"

"A bit ago, a kilo was worth two hundred yen or so, but no
it nets only half of that. Even with this much, it'll probably com
out to just over a thousand yen."

"Finding so many must be difficult."

"I've gained a dependent." Masayuki looked at Naka's ten
and forced a grin. "Have to make a living."

Natsume also turned his eyes toward the tent. "How is Nak
doing?"

"His cold won't go away."

"I see… This place has become very quiet, hasn't it," Natsu
me said, looking around.

"Because the culprit hasn't been caught. I mean, the polic
wouldn't hustle over one homeless man getting killed," Masayu
ki, his eyes fixed on Natsume, replied with sarcasm.

The detective pointed toward the plaza. "Would you lik
some tea?"

"We ascertained Sho's identity," Natsume said, handing Masayu
ki the canned coffee from the vending machine. "Real name Sho
ta Aizawa, thirty-seven years old. His parents live in Kanagaw

prefecture."

Thirty-seven—one year younger than Masayuki. "How did you find out?" he asked.

"It's a little sensitive. Could you keep it between us?"

"Yes."

"He had a criminal record. Seventeen years ago, Mr. Aizawa was involved in a manslaughter case."

Manslaughter—in other words, he'd killed someone. The moment Masayuki learned this, he felt repulsed by Sho. "Who did he kill—of course, just between us," he asked.

Natsume spoke with some hesitancy. "The victim was a nineteen-year-old office worker. On the day he got his first paycheck, he was assaulted on his way home."

"And he died as a result?"

"Yes. Apparently, they'd been in different grades at the same middle school. Mr. Aizawa had bullied the deceased man out of his money and belongings since their school days."

Hearing this reminded Masayuki of how Sho had beaten up and taken the wallets of the three youths. It seemed Sho hadn't changed at all since his teens.

"There is something I need to ask you—about the business card of a film production director that was found in Mr. Aizawa's wallet. Were you aware that he had such an acquaintance? We tried contacting the company, but they'd gone bankrupt so we couldn't talk to them…"

"He told me that he was on TV half a year ago."

"TV?"

"The usual stuff. A documentary program, slumming with the homeless. I heard they did blur his face out, though."

"I see…" Natsume growled, plunged into thought.

"What is it?"

"Well…" punted the detective.

But Masayuki had a vague idea as to what Natsume was

thinking. Perhaps it wasn't the youths who'd come to the pa
earlier, but rather the bereaved family of the office worker who
Sho had killed, who'd gotten their revenge.

It was a possibility. The bereaved had seen the documenta
and learned that Sho, who'd killed their son, now lived in Ik
bukuro as a homeless man. His face might have been blurred, b
if they knew about the tattoo on the back of his hand, they coul
have figured out it was Sho.

Masayuki's heart ached when he thought about the famil
He understood the pain of a parent whose son's life had bee
stolen away.

Because if he ever ran across the person who'd run over an
killed Tomoki…

"Hey, Masa…" Naka called from inside his sleeping bag.

"What, want a drink?" Masayuki came to his side and smile

"It's past time you said goodbye to this place," muttere
Naka.

"The hell are you saying? There's no way I could just leav
you and go."

"You can leave this old man here. I won't be living much lon
ger, but you still have many years ahead of you," Naka said wit
a fainthearted expression that was rare on him.

"So dramatic for just catching a cold…"

"You can't just keep living this life!" Naka raised his voice t
interrupt Masayuki. "Going on like this will lay waste to you
soul."

"It's already a wasteland," Masayuki muttered as Naka looke
into his eyes as if to peer into him. "I don't know what I'm livin
for…"

"Masa, do you have a family?"

"I do—no, did."

In the dim tent, Masayuki remembered his son Tomoki.

Heartless

Tomoki had passed away seven months ago after he'd just started elementary school. He'd fallen victim to a hit and run at a crosswalk.

Masayuki and his wife Saeko were stricken with grief upon losing their only child. They waited in vain for the culprit who'd run over Tomoki to be apprehended. Masayuki vented his pent-up anger and sorrow at Saeko.

Tomoki had been hit on the way home from running an errand for Saeko. It was by no means his wife's fault. He understood that well enough. In fact, he should have consoled his wife, who was already tormenting herself. But he could only come to grips with the unjust reality then by blaming Saeko.

Soon their marital relationship became stormy. On his job too, Masayuki didn't feel like working at all and started arguing frequently with his superiors and coworkers. Once he went home, a chilly evening with Saeko awaited him. Up until then, he'd only worked hard so that his wife and son could live well. He'd thought it had been his own reason for living, but now, he didn't know what he worked or lived for.

One night, Masayuki got into a shouting match with Saeko over some trifle.

The next morning, she wouldn't come out of her room even after he got up. They'd been using separate ones since Tomoki's death. He signed the divorce papers he'd obtained a few days earlier, left them on the table, and stepped out of the door.

Masayuki's work was in Otemachi. But when the train stopped at Otemachi station, he couldn't bring himself to rise from his seat. He'd felt that way ever since he'd lost Tomoki, but until now he'd somehow coaxed himself off the train. This time, however, no matter how much he encouraged himself, he couldn't stand up.

Everything could go to hell—that was his mindset.

Since then, and for the past four months, he'd been wandering homeless and jobless.

"How about your son's grave?" Naka, who'd been listenin
Masayuki, asked. He hit at a sore spot. "Are you going to bur
your wife with that?"

"Of course I'll visit."

"Living like this, are you going to steal flowers somew
there to offer your son?" When Masayuki couldn't reply, N
added, "You're a coward."

The first sharp words ever to come from the old man's mo
stung. "Yeah, I'm a coward," Masayuki admitted. "I know t
But what's more cowardly is killing someone, leaving scars,
getting away with it," he spat. He'd thought that for a while n

Masayuki was crushing aluminum cans in front of his tent w
Natsume came by. He had a shopping bag in one hand.

"Is Naka in his tent?" the detective called to Masayuki.

When he answered, "Yeah," Natsume entered the old m
abode.

Even after half an hour, the detective failed to reeme
Wondering what was happening, Masayuki peeked inside.

"Masa, why don't you join us?" invited Natsume, who
crouched in the tent. He was cooking a soup of meat, burdo
and carrots over the portable stove. Tearing off kneaded fl
dough in thin pieces, he dropped them into the pot.

Pouring some in a large bowl, he handed it to Naka, w
slurped the broth and ate with relish.

"Yum. *Suiton*, that takes me back." Of late, Naka hadn't
any appetite. It actually had to be delicious for him to be eat
so wholeheartedly.

"It's similar to *suiton*, but this is called *hittsumi*," Natsu
enlightened Naka.

"Huh, *hittsumi*. First I've heard of it," the old man marvel

Natsume had made three people's worth, and he a

Masayuki went to have theirs on a bench in the plaza.

What a strange man—that was Masayuki's thought as he glanced at Natsume, who was holding his bowl and having a mouthful of *hittsumi*.

Knowing that he was a detective didn't make him intimidating in the least. He was generous even to homeless people like them. The man was no doubt good-natured, but how did that work out for a cop? It was nice of him to treat them to a homemade meal, but was he actually investigating the case? Masayuki's positive impression of Natsume as a person nestled next to countervailing doubts.

"About the office worker you mentioned the other day... whom Sho killed," Masayuki began.

"Yes, what about it?"

"Do you think there's a possibility that one of the bereaved killed Sho?"

"I could tell you were thinking that, too," Natsume replied, looking straight at Masayuki.

"It's a possibility, isn't it."

"The day before yesterday, I went to meet with that person's father."

So Natsume did suspect the family of the man who'd been killed by Sho.

"When his son passed away, he was living in Yokohama, but now he's living alone in Shizuoka. We were able to confirm his alibi for when the case occurred."

"And the victim's mother?"

"It seems she succumbed to illness two years ago."

"Oh..."

They were able to confirm an alibi for the father—this wasn't Masayuki's problem, but he was relieved to hear it. He felt surer that the culprits were the youths who had come by the park.

"There's something I'd like you to see," Natsume said, pulling a photo from his pocket. It was of a bottle of imported whiskey. "It's the murder weapon from Mr. Aizawa's case. We found it yesterday in a trash can at another park."

Masayuki examined the photo. The bottle was covered in mud, and the bloodstains spattered on the label made it hard to read. But it said Macallan. "I don't know if this is the same one, but Sho had this brand in his shack."

"I see. I appreciate it," Natsume thanked him.

Masayuki stood up from the bench. "Are we done? I need to work."

"Just one more thing," Natsume stopped him. "How old are you, Masa?"

"I'm thirty-eight."

"The same as me. This may not be any of my business, but how long do you intend to continue this lifestyle?"

Natsume's words caught Masayuki off guard. "That really is none of your business," he replied, chewing over his irritation.

"Just earlier, I spoke with Naka about you. I can't begin to fathom the pain of losing your child. But—"

"You can't!" flared up Masayuki. "How could you know what it's like to grieve for your only son? It's not just grief. After the grief comes the helpless emptiness. I'd been hanging in there to protect my dear family. But no matter how hard I tried, someone, some stranger, could just rob me of my happiness. What am I supposed to hang in there and live for now? Let folks who're still happy bandy words like 'hard work' and 'effort'!" Masayuki spouted before heading back to his tent, as though in flight.

That night in his tent, Masayuki drank for a change. Naka's words, and Natsume's, had pierced and lodged in his heart.

He'd thought that leaving that house behind might liberate him, if only a little, from the pain of mourning. If he kept living as a drifting weed, his heart might grow numb and easy; yet, the wound in his heart had only deepened. No matter where he ran, was there no way to run from his past in the end?

Suddenly, he couldn't bear being alone. What a weak person he was. When he'd been with Saeko, her human presence had been so unbearable, but when he tried living alone, the inexorable loneliness of it nearly crushed him.

Masayuki took the bottle and headed to Naka's tent.

"Naka, let's drink together," he called from outside.

There was no response. Was he already asleep?

Oh well—if he drank right next to him, the man might eventually wake up.

Masayuki turned over the tarp and went inside. He turned on the flashlight. He poured a drink into his cup and downed it.

"Naka… I respect you. You've been living like this for ten years. Alone… Might be beyond me… If I keep living like this, I might start not wanting to live at all… Because I'm weak… Hey, say something."

Masayuki turned the light toward the sleeping bag.

He felt something was amiss and moved close to Naka's face. The area around his mouth was stained red.

The moment Masayuki saw that, his heart started beating furiously. "Naka, Naka, what's wrong!"

He shook Naka's body. The old man let out an agonized moan. In an instant, Masayuki sobered up.

While he waited sitting on a bench in the hospital hallway, a doctor approached him. Masayuki stood and bowed.

"Are you family?" the doctor asked.

"No, I'm not," Masayuki replied.

"Could you contact his relatives, then?"

"I don't know them at all. Is Naka that sick?"

"It's terminal lung cancer. How did he ever ignore it for so long? Unfortunately, there's nothing that can be done at this point. All we can do now is take measures to reduce his suffe ing..." the doctor told Masayuki and left.

Masayuki weakly sank onto the bench and hung his head.

"You're lucky. You can eat nutritious stuff while you're here," M sayuki said to Naka, who was in bed.

Two days after being brought to the hospital in an amb lance, Naka had regained consciousness. According to the docto however, he was still in an unpredictable state.

"Masa, I know you've got work to do, so don't be visitin every day," Naka said with a gentle smile.

"I'm getting it done all right. More importantly, I never ask till now but...do you have family?"

"Family... Nope, I was always alone," Naka answered with lonely little laugh.

"I see."

What would happen when Naka died? With no one but M sayuki the wiser, would he be given a quiet pauper's burial?

Masayuki almost sighed, but did his best to stifle it.

He heard a knock and turned around. The door opened an Natsume entered.

"How are you?" he asked, approaching Naka's bed.

"Pretty good. When I'm discharged, make me *hittsumi* again

"I thought you'd say that, so I cooked some." Natsume hois ed up the plastic bag in his hand. "I've checked with the nurse.

"But it's probably cold. I can go microwave it somewhere Masayuki offered.

"No need. I know many people at this hospital, so I bo rowed their kitchen and made this just now."

So that was it—Masayuki understood when he heard Natsu me's explanation.

The homeless Naka had been treated quite cordially sinc being admitted. Perhaps Natsume had put in a word with th hospital.

Extracting a large plastic bowl from his bag, Natsume placed it in front of Naka. When he opened it, steam came rising out. Natsume pulled up a folding chair and sat next to Masayuki.

Natsume watched with delight as Naka ate the *hittsumi*. When the old man finished, the detective turned to Masayuki and said, "I'd like to speak with him, just the two of us."

"In that case…" Masayuki stood up.

"It's okay. Masa, stay," Naka begged, exchanging looks with Natsume. "Please."

Hearing this, the detective closed his eyes. He seemed to be thinking over something. When he opened his eyes, he looked at Naka and asked, "Are you sure?"

"Yup… Please."

"I understand… We found out who murdered Mr. Aiza-wa—"

"Oh?! You mean…you caught those guys?" Masayuki, surprised, turned to look at Natsume, who sat down next to him.

But not meeting his gaze, Natsume instead stared at Naka and continued, "The fingerprints we found on the bottle used as the murder weapon matched the ones from the cup and bowl in your tent. You're the one who killed Mr. Aizawa, yes?"

Appalled, Masayuki looked back and forth at the two's faces.

What was the man saying? There was no way Naka was the—

"Yes."

Masayuki's eyes widened at the reply. "Why? Why would you kill Sho?"

"Looking at that guy started to piss me off. You remember that night, don't you? Calling me a geezer, talking big…"

"But, just for that… I don't believe it," Masayuki appealed to Naka.

"Masa, I told you the other day, didn't I? Living this life lays waste to your soul over time. If you get that, hurry up and wash your hands of it," Naka told Masayuki off with a cutting look. Then, staring at Natsume: "You've been good to me. I don't want to cause you too much trouble. I'm ready to go to prison or anywhere."

"Please, the truth," Natsume demanded, meeting his gaze.

"The truth?" Naka knit his eyebrows.

"You aren't Naka, or Yasutaro Nakajima, but rather Yukihiko Motoki, the father of Yukiya Motoki whom Mr. Aizawa killed, yes?"

Naka shook his head. "Motoki? Who's that… I don't even know anyone by that name."

"You probably saw the documentary Mr. Aizawa appeared in half a year ago. Even though his face was blurred out, you knew it was him from the tattoo on the back of his hand. Having learned that Mr. Aizawa was living homeless in Ikebukuro, you cast everything aside and chose to be close to him. In Tokyo, you sought out a homeless man your age and appearance and asked him if he wanted to trade places. That person was Yasutaro Nakajima, who'd always lived in Aomori but had come to the capital recently."

"On what evidence are you—"

"I have evidence," Natsume interrupted Naka. "Yasutaro Nakajima has a past, a record of three cases of assault. Running the fingerprints is all it takes," the detective shut down Naka, who looked dumbstruck.

"Naka. You became homeless on purpose to get revenge on Sho?" Masayuki asked plaintively.

Naka didn't try to answer.

"I doubt it…" Natsume spoke instead. "You probably didn't become homeless intending to kill him. You wanted to know how he was living now, how he'd come to terms with the guilt of having killed your son. Yes?"

Naka replied with a small nod. "Yeah…I didn't start living

this way in order to kill him. If I'd meant to…I'd have tracked him down sooner. How much easier that would've been. Since Yukiya was killed, my wife and I bore a pain like our hearts were being torn apart. Even then, we somehow propped each other up and went on living. Times like that, only family who're sharing the same suffering can support one another."

Naka glanced at Masayuki, and Saeko's face flashed in his mind.

"But my wife's been dead for two years now…and when I got sick half a year ago and went to the hospital, they told me that I had lung cancer," Naka offered up with sagging shoulders.

Masayuki glanced at Natsume's profile. The detective was gazing at the man as he told his story.

"The doctor didn't tell me exactly how many months I had to live, but I sensed that it wasn't for long. I'd already lost my wife, my son. I thought about going to a hospice and spending my remaining days there. That's when, by chance, I found out about that guy from television. At first, I just wanted to witness, before I died, the miserable life of the man who'd killed Yukiya. I started living as a homeless in Ikebukuro and, while looking for that guy, met Yasutaro Nakajima. Maybe because we're the same generation, he treated me kindly. Although he wanted to go on experiencing life, he was in a position where living wasn't easy. I was going to die soon. Thinking about that, I made a decision. To be by that guy up until the brink of death. If, during that time, I saw even the slightest bit of humanity or conscience in him, it might save me a little…"

"And so you changed places with Nakajima."

"I gave him conditions for the trade. I'd sell my house and hand him what was left of my assets. He'd go someplace else but offer proper memorial services for my wife and son's graves going forward."

"Wait, if you did that, you wouldn't be buried with your wife and son," Masayuki pointed out.

"I was prepared for that. If I died, I'd already be with my wife and son," Naka said with a mournful look. "But even after seventeen years, that guy hadn't changed one bit. That night… Beating up the kids who launched fireworks at the tents, he said, 'I wouldn't give a shit if I beat you bloody and killed you'—then took their money. He talked like having nothing to lose was something to be proud of, like he didn't even register or regret having robbed someone of something dear… At that point, the pent-up anger that I'd desperately held back exploded."

"So you murdered Mr. Aizawa, who went back to his tent and to bed, by clubbing his head with a bottle."

"Right… Considering the state my body is in, I might as well have confessed to the police. But…I wanted to be with Masa just a little longer… It almost feels like I'm hanging out with a grown-up version of my son…" Naka cast a lonely look at Masayuki. "Thank you for everything…"

Masayuki welled up with tears at the words.

"At any rate…" Naka sighed. "I thought we'd thoroughly gone over each other's circumstances at the outset… To think that he had priors…"

Natsume stood up and placed a photo in front of Naka. It showed three people, who appeared to be Naka, his wife, and his son. "It was difficult to find. You must have disposed of all the photos you had."

Naka held the photo and looked at it with longing. "When did you start suspecting me?" he asked.

"When we first met, I asked you your name and birthplace. Running your background check at the station afterwards, I had my doubts. Mr. Nakajima had priors for assault and battery, but you told me about yourself candidly and without hesitation. I thought someone with priors who's questioned by the police should tend to demur, at least to some degree, loath to draw attention to his record."

"I see..." Naka grinned wryly.

"It was after I made *hittsumi* in your tent that I felt certain."

Naka looked at the empty bowl before him. "This dish?"

"*Hittsumi* is a famous local specialty in southern Aomori. If you lived in Hachinoe, then you should have known it."

"You really got me there."

"No, at the time, I really just wanted you to have a meal from back home and get better," Natsume clarified. "The one thing I couldn't figure out is why we suddenly found the murder weapon. After the crime, you must have buried the bottle that served as the murder weapon. Why bother to dig it up and toss it in another park's trash bin..."

"Even a fine detective can have one puzzle he can't solve," Naka said with an air of mystery.

But Masayuki knew the answer. *What's more cowardly is killing someone, leaving scars, and getting away with it*—his words back then must have led Naka to that decision.

"Going so far for the murder of a mere homeless guy..." Naka said, turning to him. "Police aren't anything to spit at, eh, Masa."

"No person is a 'mere' anything," chided Natsume.

"True..." Naka mouthed the word as though savoring it. "Maybe I didn't just lose a house to live in back then, but also my heart. When I die, I wonder if I'll go to the same place as my wife and son," he asked Natsume.

"I hope you do." Looking straight at the old man, the detective nodded slowly.

Masayuki headed to the elevator alongside Natsume.

"Oh, Mr. Natsume," a passing nurse called out. "Are you visiting Emi?"

"No, not today," Natsume answered, heading on to the

elevator.

"Who's this Emi?" Masayuki asked.

"My daughter is hospitalized here."

"Why don't you visit her, then?" Masayuki said.

Natsume thought about it for a bit, nodded, and replied, "Right."

Deciding that he might as well also go, Masayuki followed after him.

They rode the elevator and walked down a hall; Natsume stopped in front of a room.

Natsume knocked and opened the door. A girl was sleeping on the bed. A whole bunch of dolls lay by her side.

"Emi, how are you doing?" Natsume approached the bed and affectionately stroked the girl's hair. She didn't react to his words at all. Masayuki wondered if she was asleep, but after watching for a bit, he sensed that that wasn't the case. A tube protruded from the girl's nose.

After talking to her about many things, Natsume came back towards Masayuki and told the completely unresponsive girl, "I'll come again," before quietly closing the door.

They rode the elevator and proceeded toward the exit.

"What's wrong with her?" Masayuki asked, unable not to.

"She's been like that since she got hit in the head with a hammer."

Natsume's words came as a shock. "Hit with a hammer, by who?"

"Ten years ago, there was a case involving a serial assailant who targeted toddlers near this area. Before I started this job," Natsume said, biting his lip.

"The culprit?"

"Hasn't been caught."

How could you know what it's like to grieve for your only son?

Masayuki had uttered those words to a man who was quite

familiar with such circumstances.

"What am I supposed to hang in there and live for now? You said that at some point. Frankly, I have no idea, either, and haven't these last ten years. What I'm supposed to hang in there and live for. But Masa—" Natsume turned an impassioned gaze towards him. "We'll stand firm, won't we?"

Pride

So that's the crime scene—

Wataru Nagamine spotted the patrol cars parked in front of the condominium and decelerated.

He got out of his car and looked around to see many onlookers gathered outside the cordoning tape.

"Nagamine, Investigation Section One." Flashing his police badge at a uniformed officer, he passed under the tape. Once in the condominium, he headed to Room 308, which had been turned into a crime scene.

A length of tape barred entry to Room 308, too. To the side, a suited man was listening to a young woman and taking notes. He was likely a detective from the local precinct.

"I'm Nagamine from Investigation Section One," Nagamine called out to the man. "Can we go in?"

"Thanks for your trouble. Forensics is done, so yes."

Nagamine put on white gloves and the shoe covers deposited inside the front door and made his way into the apartment.

On the right side was the kitchen, and on the left, the bathroom. Ahead was a medium-sized, Western-style room. Subsection Chief Yabusawa was standing next to a bed that lay along the wall.

When Nagamine called out "Cheers," Yabusawa turned around, parroted the greeting, and immediately looked back at the bed.

Nagamine approached him and cast his eyes on the dead

woman on it.

Beneath her open bathrobe, she was stark naked. Her age… late twenties? Bringing his face close to hers, he saw that it was engorged with blood and that her eyes showed signs of hemorrhaging. He could also identify choke marks on her neck.

Strangulation, then—

"A crime of passion…or thereabouts."

"Likely," Yabusawa said and pointed at a trash can in the corner. "We found a used condom. Hopefully the lady wasn't too loose…but do question the tenants in this complex for the time being."

When Nagamine exited the room with that order from Yabusawa, his eyes met with the detective who'd been speaking with a woman.

Had he met the man somewhere before? Nagamine thought he recognized his face.

"I'm Natsume from the East Ikebukuro station. This is Ms. Watanabe, who discovered the body."

Even after hearing the man's name, Nagamine couldn't remember. "Could you share your account with me, too?" he requested of Watanabe, and the agitated woman related the conditions in which she found the victim.

The victim's name was Ayano Sakurai—

Even though Ayano had important work that day at the Ikebukuro travel agency which employed her, she never showed up. There was a business matter that only Ayano knew about, so they called her to get her immediate confirmation but couldn't reach her. Since Ayano was never late or absent without permission, Watanabe visited her room fearing that her colleague was sick.

"And when you arrived, the door was unlocked?" Nagamine asked, to which Watanabe nodded and replied, "Yes…"

"We'll likely ask you to tell us again at the station, thank you. Detective Natsume…can we do these interviews together?"

Nagamine and Natsume went around the condominium questioning the tenants.

Both next-door neighbors were out. Although two residents on the third floor were able to oblige, they hadn't noticed anything particularly unusual.

"Now that you mention it… Last night, I heard something like an argument from downstairs," testified the resident in Room 408.

"Around what time?"

"What time was it… Hmmm… Around nine, I think?"

Nagamine looked over his shoulder. Natsume was taking it down. "Do you remember what they were talking about?" Nagamine pressed.

"I don't really remember… It was a high-pitched woman's voice… 'Who're you to be blaming me?' or something along those lines, I think… Sounded like a lovers' quarrel."

A crime of passion, after all—

An investigation headquarters was established in the East Ikebukuro station assembly hall, and the detectives filtered in.

"Excuse me."

Nagamine raised his face at the voice to see Natsume standing there. The man sat down next to him.

Was he going to be Nagamine's buddy until investigation headquarters was dissolved?

"Natsume… Had we met before at some other crime scene?" Nagamine asked what had been bothering him.

Natsume seemed lost in thought for some time.

"What about before here?" Nagamine had never handled an East Ikebukuro precinct case until now. Maybe it had been in a different jurisdiction.

"No, I've always been at East Ikebukuro."

This was surprising. Nagamine had assumed that they were

the same generation, but maybe Natsume was much younger than he looked.

"How old are you?"

"Thirty-eight."

The same age as Nagamine—but serving at the same station until you were thirty-eight was rare.

Sensing his doubt, Natsume explained, "I entered the police academy when I was thirty."

"Ah…okay."

"I'd been in the community section, but I was assigned to the detective unit a year ago."

So the guy was a rookie.

An underwhelming buddy—but all Nagamine had to do was take the initiative in the investigation as usual.

The chiefs came into the assembly hall and the investigation meeting began.

"The victim's name is Ayano Sakurai—twenty-six years old—an office worker at the Ikebukuro branch of a travel agency called Try Travel," Yabusawa began describing the case.

The cause of death was suffocation by strangulation. Estimated time of death, between seven and ten o'clock the previous evening.

Ayano had been living in that condominium for a year. Since the complex had a gated intercom system, and because they couldn't find her cellphone in her room, it was highly likely that the crime was committed by someone she knew.

The semen from the condom left in the room and the hair left in the bathroom would be submitted for DNA testing.

With a directive to pay particular attention to Ayano's social life, the meeting was adjourned.

As ordered by Yabusawa, Nagamine and Natsume immediately went to the travel agency to gather information from Ayano's coworkers.

They were shown through to the office, and after a while, the manager of the branch made his appearance.

"To think that...Sakurai would be involved in a case like this," the manager, who sat across from Nagamine and Natsume, began speaking, barely able to hide his discomposure.

"What sort of woman was Ms. Sakurai?" Nagamine asked.

"A serious one. She performed her work diligently and, of course, was never late or took days off without permission. It hadn't even been a full year since she started, but we could trust her with important work..."

"Do you know what she did before working here?"

"She worked at another travel agency in Iidabashi."

"So in the same industry. Do you know why she changed jobs?"

"No...I didn't pry that much. Well, she came from the same industry, and we hired her because she would be an immediate asset."

"We would like to ask you about Ms. Sakurai's social circle..." Nagamine turned the talk to Ayano's friendships and romantic relationships.

The manager, however, answered, "I wouldn't know much about that..." and instead called in the staff in attendance one by one.

"Was there a man she was dating?" Nagamine asked Ayano's coworkers, but every one of them replied that they never really discussed such matters with her.

"Should we go to her old workplace?" he said to Natsume as they exited Try Travel, and together they headed toward Iidabashi.

All Skies Travel was a small company along Mejiro Street in Iidabashi.

"Welcome."

When they entered the store, there were three employees behind the counter.

"We apologize for coming at a busy time. I am Nagamine from the Metropolitan Police Department." He showed them his police badge, and they stared at him with wide eyes. "We would like to ask you about Ayano Sakurai, who was employed here previously."

The woman right in front of him gave a doubtful look and said, "About Ayano?"

"Yes. Actually…Ms. Sakurai was involved in a case last night…"

"A case…" the woman, who was staring at Nagamine, asked anxiously.

"She was murdered," he informed her.

She was speechless. The next moment, she angrily stood up. "That can't be true!"

"Unfortunately, it is. Someone strangled and murdered her. We are conducting the investigation and have some questions regarding Ms. Sakurai."

Though flustered, the woman nodded and offered them seats at the counter.

"How long have you known Ms. Sakurai?" Nagamine asked as he sat in the chair.

"We worked together for about two years."

"Were you close to her outside of the office?"

"While she was still working here, we went out for meals together, sometimes for drinks…but I didn't see her much after she left…"

"Why did she resign?" Nagamine asked, but the woman wasn't forthcoming. She seemed of two minds about telling him.

"Please answer honestly so that we can catch the murderer."

"She…was being troubled by a stalker," the woman answered.

"A stalker?"

"Yes...she was being bothered by someone she'd gone out with ages ago. She'd dated him for about a year, but apparently he was really violent... It seemed she'd broken up with him because of that, but even afterwards, he wouldn't stop trying to get in bed with her... He kept visiting her place, and yelling outside, and even came here... Once, he stayed all day over there across the street and just gazed into the store."

She pointed in Nagamine's direction, so he turned around. Beyond the glass door he could see Mejiro Street.

"Do you know that man's name?"

"I think... Kamiya... I believe it was Kamiya."

Natsume took down the name.

"Do you know his given name?"

"I'm sorry, I don't know that much... But she quit this place because she couldn't stand being followed by him."

"And that was one year ago, correct?" Nagamine asked, to which she nodded.

It had also been one year ago that Ayano had moved into her present condominium. Thanks to the man, she must have needed to find a new home, too.

"Do you know this man's workplace or where he lives?"

"I have no idea where he works, but I heard that he lives in Narimasu. She'd been working at a travel agency in Narimasu before here, so I guess they might have met there. 'I never have luck with men,' she always said."

"Luck with men..."

"Yes. It seems that it wasn't just that man, all the ones she'd dated were good for nothing, and she wondered if she were somehow to blame... Even when she left this place, she was saying, 'I'm done with men.'"

The crime scene seemed to suggest, however, that she wasn't.

"Once she quit, you didn't see her much?"

"I was worried about her in the days after she left, and we

sent each other messages, but we lost touch... Oh, but around two weeks ago, I ran into her in Ikebukuro."

"Is that right?"

"Yes...and we went into a department store cafe. She seemed very cheerful compared to those days, so I was relieved."

"What did you talk about? For instance, did she tell you about any man in her life, about friends?"

"She said she had a new boyfriend."

"What kind of man?" Nagamine leaned forward and asked.

"Umm, she didn't tell me about how they met and all that, but she said he was manly. She gushed about him. 'He really understands me... He'd protect me with his life... He's the manliest person I've ever met.'"

If this had been two weeks ago, he was likely Ayano's latest lover.

"But..." The woman paused there.

"But what?"

"Well... When I told her I was happy to hear about it, she said something like... 'I love him so much I can't stand it, but... maybe it's not meant to be.'"

Not meant to be—was it perhaps an adulterous relationship?

An affair and break-up gone wrong... Nagamine painted the scenario in his head.

"Would you know the man's name?"

"Now that you ask, right in the middle of our conversation, she took a call from someone she called Kai. I'm not sure if he was the boyfriend... But given how happy she looked talking to him, probably... And now I'll never see her again," she concluded in a wistful murmur.

Kai—they could be in luck if they could figure out who it was from Ayano's call records.

The car turned left at Kawagoe Way and onto Kanpachi Road.

Having left All Skies Travel, they were headed toward the apartment in Kasugacho, Nerima Ward where Ayano had lived up until a year ago.

Looking out at the familiar streets from the passenger's seat, he sank into gloomy thoughts. Nearly ten years ago, he'd combed through this neighborhood until he was sick and tired of it.

It had fallen prey to a serial assailant who targeted little girls. It was Nagamine's first major case since being assigned to Investigation Section One.

In succession, two girls had been hit in the head with a hammer while playing alone, one of them passing away.

Eyewitness reports indicated that the culprit was a boy of about fifteen or sixteen. Despite a thorough investigation of the neighborhood, he was never apprehended. The case was handed over to an ongoing investigations unit but was probably not one step closer to being solved.

"I don't like this neighborhood much…" he muttered to himself.

"Me neither…"

Nagamine turned toward the driver's seat in response.

"Up until ten years ago, I lived near here."

Natsume's profile, as the man stared straight ahead and drove, sent a certain image flitting across his mind.

He'd seen it on TV at the precinct station. The victim's father, tears in his eyes, desperately pleading to the culprit—

One of the victims was called Emi Natsume.

Natsume—could the person next to him possibly be the victim's father from back then?

But he'd never heard that the victim's father was on the force. No, he was sure he'd been told that the father worked at a juvenile detention center.

I entered the police academy when I was thirty—

What, had he joined because of that case?

His gaze fixed on Natsume's profile, Nagamine was unable to find his next words.

At Ayano's old apartment, they interviewed her former next-door neighbor.

"True… A weird fellow did keep coming by. He'd kick the door and shout in the middle of the night…a real nuisance," the male resident said with a fed-up look.

"Have you seen that man since she left?"

"Yeah, I've seen him around a number of times even afterwards."

"Even after she moved away?"

"He was probably looking for her friend."

"Her friend?"

"Yeah. Just the other day too, right by that convenience store, I saw her being grilled by that guy. It was like she was getting threatened for something, and I felt bad for her." His insouciant tone contradicted his professed sympathy.

"What's this friend like?"

"She didn't try to stand out, little or no makeup… Seemed to come here often, too, when my neighbor was still living here. I bet this friend was being harassed because he thought she knew the woman's new address. But a guy who threatens a weak girl, he's scum, yeah?"

In that case, he definitely should have called the police or tried to help her, but Nagamine let that thought go unvoiced.

"Does this woman live close by?"

"I would think so. I've seen her a few other times, too… Strange thing is, she has a different hairstyle every time I spot her. When I saw her here, she had a short haircut, but other times she had long black hair."

"It must be a wig."

"That must be it… She was pretty tall and slim, and I thought she might actually be a model."

That woman might know about Ayano's latest boyfriend, too.

"Thank you very much."

Leaving the apartment, he went back to the car with Natsume. His wristwatch said that it was past six in the evening. "Should we go back to the station?" he suggested, but when he got into the car, Natsume, who was in the driver's seat, had a despondent look on his face.

"What's wrong?" Nagamine asked.

"Well... There's one point that's bothering me."

"What?"

"I was wondering, if she was so scared of Kamiya, why did she only move as far away as Ikebukuro? If Narimasu is where Kamiya lives, wouldn't he show up in Ikebukuro often enough? They might actually run into each other. Too bad she didn't move farther away."

He had a point, but—"I don't see how that's relevant to this case."

Natsume didn't look convinced but nodded slightly and turned the key.

Several new pieces of information were aired in the evening investigation meeting.

Ayano had changed her cellphone a year ago, and her new one didn't have the name Kamiya in its call record. The meeting ended after it was decided that several investigators including Nagamine would contact the people in the call record the next day.

"Your daughter..." he called out to Natsume's back as the man was leaving the assembly hall.

Natsume turned around and stared curiously at Nagamine.

"I always felt like we'd met somewhere before, but I only realized earlier today. Natsume... You're the victim's father from that case, aren't you."

"My daughter is still in the hospital."

Still in the hospital…

"She hasn't regained consciousness since then."

So she was a vegetable. He couldn't find the right words.

"By any chance, were you part of the investigation for that case?"

"Yeah…it was a humiliating experience."

"You mean 'is'."

For the victims' families, the case would never slip into the past. Natsume's eyes said as much.

"Right…it's still possible."

While he could no longer conduct an investigation himself, it wasn't as though no means for catching the culprit existed.

The assailant had left behind a definitive clue. A glove had been discarded near the second crime scene. Bloodstains from the victim on the outside pretty much proved that it had been used by the culprit. He'd been careful about fingerprints but seemed not to have realized that his sweat would be left inside. As long as they had that DNA, even now, ten years later, they could still identify him.

"You…became a cop so you can arrest the perp?" Nagamine asked, hardly able to believe it.

"It's not so that *I* can… The police must apprehend the perpetrator of that case. Isn't that so?"

Natsume's eyes seem to glint.

The next day, Nagamine and Natsume headed to a door-to-door delivery service distribution center in Minami-Otsuka.

They went to meet with a person in Ayano's cellphone records, a Shoichi Kaitani. At 6:15 on the night of the incident, Kaitani had called Ayano. Kaitani was twenty-eight with a wife and children.

Kai—they needed to meet him in person first, but Nagamine thought that the chances of Kaitani being Ayano's lover were high.

At the front desk, when they explained the reasons for their visit, they were escorted to the parking lot where Kaitani was.

"Mr. Kaitani—there are police here to see you," the receptionist said, and Kaitani, who had been moving packages to his truck, looked at them with a start. His short, stout build and behavior was reminiscent of a certain fainthearted bear character.

"We are sorry for bothering you at such a busy time."

As they showed him their badges and approached him, Kaitani met them with obvious fear on his face.

"We are here to ask you about Ms. Ayano Sakurai."

"What about her?"

No matter how desperately he tried to retain his composure, they could clearly see he was flustered.

"Did you know about the incident Ms. Sakurai was involved in?"

"Yes… I found out through the news yesterday. I was surprised… Such a thing happening to her…" His body was trembling.

"What kind of relationship did you have with Ms. Sakurai?"

"What kind?" He seemed at a loss for an answer. "We were just acquaintances…"

"Since when?"

"I-I wonder since when… I-It must have been about two months back, I think. We were introduced by my coworker Ms. Aikawa…"

Ms. Aikawa—that had to be Miu Aikawa, who worked at the same delivery company. Miu was also in Ayano's call records.

"I was drinking at a bar in Ikebukuro. Ms. Aikawa and Ms. Sakurai happened to be drinking nearby, so that day we all got together and…"

"And after that?"

"We messaged each other on our phones a few times...just chatting a little..."

"One day prior...the night of the incident, that is, you contacted Ms. Sakurai, is that right?"

Kaitani turned pale.

"What business did you have with her?"

"It wasn't anything... I just...asked how she was..."

"Is that true? After that, did you not go to her condominium?"

He shook his head. "I didn't go, I didn't."

"Where were you yesterday, between the hours of seven and eleven at night?"

"I don't really remember...but I finished work and...wandered around Ikebukuro. I went into the department store and read in a bookshop..."

He thought it was a lie, but at least asked which store Kaitani had stopped by.

"Excuse me...are you almost done? I won't be able to meet my deadline."

Kaitani hurriedly loaded the packages and got into his truck. Nagamine watched it drive away.

Enough for today. But next time they'd bring hard proof.

"That was suspicious..." he whispered to Natsume, who stood next to him.

"Shall we go see Ms. Aikawa as well?" Natsume said, then inquired at the reception desk after Miu Aikawa.

When they went to a different parking lot, they arrived as Miu was loading her truck.

"Ms. Aikawa, there are police here to see you," the receptionist called to her, to which Miu turned around.

As far as her appearance went, she was likely the friend witnessed near Ayano's apartment. A hat covered Miu's short hair.

After casting a glance at them, she pulled the hat down over her tapered, makeup-less eyes and approached them. "Is this about Ayano's case?" she asked.

"That's right... We have some things we would like to ask you about Ms. Sakurai."

"If it's to arrest the culprit, I'll answer any question... But I don't have much time, so can we do this while I work?"

"Yes," Nagamine answered, and Miu started loading the truck with packages.

She braced herself in order to lift what looked to be a heavy cardboard box. She was probably about five feet five. She was a little taller than the average woman, and he could tell, even through her work clothes, that she was slim.

"Those look too heavy for a woman's arms. Let me help."

As Nagamine put his hands on one of the boxes, she scowled, "Thanks but no thanks."

What was it with this woman? He'd only tried to help. She was headstrong—

"You came to talk about Ayano, didn't you?"

Indeed. This was hardly pleasant; he ought to just ask what he needed to and move on to the next person. "Were you close to Ms. Ayano?"

"Well, yes. We met each other now and then and called and messaged each other..."

"Since when have you known her?"

"It might have been a little over a year ago that I first got to know her..."

"What brought you together?"

"She lived near me."

So that was it—"In Kasugacho."

"Yes... We were the same age...so naturally we grew close..."

Just the other day too, right by that convenience store, I saw her being grilled by that guy—

"Do you know a man named Kamiya?"

"Yeah, I know him. The stalker guy, right? He's a disgrace to men."

"You were threatened by Kamiya too, weren't you? He wanted you to tell him Ms. Sakurai's new address?"

"You're a great detective, to know that."

Perhaps Miu had told him Ayano's new address and Kamiya had gone to the condominium that night. "Did you tell him her address?"

"I wouldn't."

"Is that the truth? We would understand if a fragile woman like you got scared, threatened by a man. Even then you aren't to blame. Please tell us the truth so that we can catch the culprit."

Miu faced them. She glared at Nagamine. "No matter what, I wouldn't betray someone dear to me," she said, her eyes filled with contempt.

"Did Ms. Sakurai tell you anything about who she was dating?" Natsume took a step forward and asked.

"I hadn't heard anything about that from Ayano."

"It seems Ms. Sakurai was dating a man called Kai. Does that name ring a bell?"

"No..."

"Are you close to Mr. Kaitani?"

"Not particularly... But compared to others at this company, we talk more."

"Would you say that Ms. Sakurai and Mr. Kaitani had been dating? We didn't ask him directly, but we got that impression..."

Miu fixed her gaze on Natsume. Eventually, she laughed out loud. "No way," she answered, swinging her hand back and forth and saying that it was impossible.

"Is it because Mr. Kaitani is a married man?"

Natsume intently watched Miu.

"Ayano wouldn't settle for just any man."

"Is that so... We're sorry for taking your time. I have just one last question for you. Where were you last night, between seven and ten?"

"At a gym near Mejiro station."

"You mean a fitness club?"

"No... A boxing gym."

"A driver for a delivery service and boxing, when you're a woman. You're one hell of a tomboy," Nagamine ribbed her.

"Detective, you should watch what you say." Miu glared at him again.

"Hey, it was just a joke."

"A joke can still cut deep into someone's heart... Are we about done," she turned her gaze away from Nagamine and asked Natsume.

"Yes... Thank you for your time and trouble."

Miu headed to the driver's seat of the truck.

"Oh, sorry, just one more question... Do you live alone in Kasugacho?"

"No... I live with my mother. After we lost my father in high school, it's just been the two of us. What about it?"

"Nothing... No particular significance."

Watching Miu's truck drive away, Nagamine clucked his tongue. "What a headstrong woman. Pisses me—"

"There are many kinds of people in the world. Shall we?" Natsume said and started walking.

"A day ago... A day ago..." The gym manager traced the attendance sheets along the wall with his finger. "Ahh, Aikawa was here. Well, I did check to make sure, but she comes almost every day to the gym to practice."

"Okay." Natsume nodded and looked around the interior.

Seeing the folks here punching sand bags and sparring in the ring seemed to tickle the fellow.

Seeing his partner like this, Nagamine wondered if the sudden suggestion to visit the gym hadn't been made out of sheer personal interest.

By the time they'd finished hitting Ayano's acquaintances, it had been past five in the afternoon. He'd meant to go back to the station from there, but Natsume had proposed out of the blue that they confirm Miu's alibi.

"How about we get going? It's almost time for the investigation meeting," he said looking at his wristwatch, but Natsume told the manager, "Please let us take a bit more of your time."

Have it your way, Nagamine spat silently, sitting on a fold-up chair beside him.

"When did Ms. Aikawa start coming to this gym?" Natsume asked the manager.

"If I remember correctly...about one year ago. At first I thought she came because of that 'boxercise' diet, but she's so passionate about practicing. Great progress over the year. I told her she has what it takes, that she should try out for the pro test, and yet...she doesn't seem to be interested at all."

"Come to think of it, they green-lighted women's pro boxing."

"Right, right... At this gym, we've got Puma Asami who's ranked high in Japan, but... Well, speak of the devil."

He looked at the front entrance, towards a woman wearing a sauna suit who'd come back from roadwork. She entered straight into the ring, mixed in with the male trainees, and started shadow boxing. Her quick footwork put the men to shame as she threw out her punches.

"If Aikawa became a pro, she'd be a good match for Asami, though..." the manager lamented.

"Why did Ms. Aikawa start boxing?" Natsume asked, returning his gaze to the manager from Puma Asami, who was still up in the ring.

"She just said she wanted to become strong… She always says she wants to become stronger. I don't know what's driving her, but…the first time she came to this gym, she had a bruise on her face. I'm not sure how she got it… Well, she's a woman so…I thought maybe something had happened…but it's not the kind of thing you pry about."

One year ago—a bruise on her face—

Maybe Kamiya had left Miu memories of something even more detestable than his threats.

No matter what, I wouldn't betray someone dear to me—

Nagamine remembered the hateful look that Miu had given him.

Nagamine and Natsume were watching Kaitani from the shadows. He was sitting at a park bench and drinking a can of juice.

Kaitani threw the can into the trash and headed out of the park, toward his truck.

"Let's," Nagamine said, and hustled to the trashcan. He put on gloves and pulled out the can carefully so that he was not touching its rim.

"I didn't kill her!"

Kaitani's cry echoed in the interrogation room.

Glancing backward, Nagamine made eye contact with Natsume, who was writing the report by the door.

"You can't talk your way out of this. Your DNA matches the semen and hair we found in Ms. Sakurai's room. How do you explain that?" Nagamine demanded, staring at Kaitani.

"Because…because… I admit that I went to Ms. Sakurai's room that night. I admit that I was in a relationship with her that I shouldn't have been in. But after we had sex, I took a shower and left right after. A month ago, we met by chance at Ikebukuro and had a drink. She was wasted, so I walked her home and I ended up in bed with her on an impulse. After that, we had those kinds of relations a few times…but I didn't kill her!"

"If you had nothing to feel guilty about, why weren't you honest about it when we met before?"

"We're talking about an affair, I did feel guilty. I really wanted to tell you the truth when you came, but I was afraid of my wife finding out… More than that, if you found out I'd been in her room right before she was killed, you'd suspect me of killing her…"

"I don't buy it. Maybe Ayano Sakurai pressured you to marry her? Or maybe she threatened to tell your wife about the affair… and then you got into an argument—"

"That's not true! It was just a whim on my part, but it was the same for her, too. She didn't think anything of me. She had someone she was dating. Someone called Kai—she told me about him a lot while we were drinking."

"What are you saying? You're Kai."

"That's not true. She wasn't in love with me. She said Kai was a much more wonderful man than me… She must have been thinking of him even while I was screwing her."

"If she had such a wonderful boyfriend, then why would she cheat with you?"

"I'm not sure myself why she would… Maybe something about him didn't satisfy her? That day, right when I was leaving, she told me, 'Let's make this the last time.' That was my intention too. Even when I was screwing her, she didn't seem the least bit happy. It hurt to look at that expression, as a man… So I said, 'I understand. Bye…' Anyway, I didn't kill her!" Kaitani appealed for all he was worth.

"How did it go?" Yabusawa, who was standing in the hallway, asked as they exited the interrogation room.

"He wouldn't admit to it."

"I see—should we have someone else try?"

Nagamine slumped his shoulders and headed to the assembly hall. "What do you think?" he asked Natsume, who was walking beside him.

"Hard to say… But he seems like a far cry from 'the manliest person I'd ever met' whom Ms. Sakurai spoke of."

"They say don't judge a book by its cover, though."

"They do, don't they? Don't judge a book by its cover." Natsume halted, turned to him, and invited, "Can we go test that out?"

With an intent look, Natsume headed on toward the stairs.

"Hey, what is this about?!" Nagamine hollered, realizing that they'd come to the boxing gym.

"Times like these, we need to blow some steam," Natsume said innocently, tugging on Nagamine's sleeve.

"Don't test me. It's almost time for the investigation meeting!" he yelled pointing to his wristwatch, but Natsume dragged him into the gym heedlessly.

The guy was messing around with him, damn it.

"Oh, the detectives from the other day. Do you have something you need?" the manager called to them as they entered the gym.

"Is Ms. Aikawa taking today off?" Natsume asked, looking around.

"She's doing roadwork right now."

"I see." Natsume stepped up to a sandbag and displayed some nimble footwork.

"Detective, you've got talent," the manager said, admiring his movements.

"Youthful follies. I dabbled in it a bit while I was a student."

"Amateur boxing, huh."

"I might not look it, but I did come in third in my prefecture once."

"In that case, why don't you try hitting it?"

The manager gave Natsume a pair of gloves. He took off his jacket and put them on. With an animated expression he'd never shown to Nagamine, he started hitting the sandbag.

Observing the man's moves, Nagamine bought that Natsume was no ordinary amateur. As a detective, however, the guy was below amateurish, he thought bitterly.

"Do you have some business with me?"

He turned around to find Miu, who'd returned from road-work, standing there.

It was Natsume who replied, "No…not really. I just wanted to exercise my body since it's been a while."

"This detective apparently boxed when he was a student. He says he was once third in his prefecture. No wonder his footwork is good."

"Oh…"

Miu went to another sandbag without showing much interest.

"Hey, Miu—" Puma Asami, who'd been practicing up in the ring, called to her. "Care to be my sparring partner for a bit?"

"No… Sorry, but I'll pass."

"Tsk, coward," Asami snorted. She left the ring and went upstairs.

Miu seemed to be biting back her chagrin. With a sharp gaze aimed at the sandbag, she started hitting it.

"Ms. Aikawa—" Natsume called to Miu, who stopped moving and faced him. "Would you spar with me?"

Holy—what was he thinking? She was a woman.

"Detective, that's a little…" the manager balked at this, too.

"Maybe we shouldn't," Natsume said to stir her up.

The mocking look he was directing at Miu made Nagamine wonder. He'd thought of his partner as a correct sort until now, but was he actually mean-spirited?

"Sounds like fun." Miu put on headgear and got up into the ring. "In exchange, no pulling punches."

"Of course."

The manager, who'd been fretting, seemed to resign himself and put headgear on Natsume. "Only one round, then."

What was Natsume thinking? What was he getting out of this?

The difference in their frames was manifest. Miu was twice as slender as Natsume and then some. Even her chest was flat, and she looked like a boy. There was also a considerable height difference.

Miu said they weren't to pull any punches, but she probably thought they were fooling around.

But when the gong sounded, Natsume moved in ferociously. Without a hint of hesitation, he landed sharp punches all over Miu's face and body.

The manager, of course, and the other trainees gazed at the ring in shock.

Miu, who hadn't been able to counterattack at all, swiveled and escaped to Natsume's back. The moment he turned around, she lay one into his torso. Natsume doubled over and paused for a moment. Immediately, with magnificent footwork, she treated his face to an upper cut.

Reversing his disadvantage in a second, Natsume slammed his fist into Miu's own face next. Fresh blood flew from her nose, but instead of circling to his back, she sent punches into his body and chin. The sound of creaking flesh resounded through the gym. It was a fierce exchange of blows—

The gong sounded, and suddenly they stopped. They each moved back to their opposite corners.

When Miu took off her headgear, her face was flushed a bright red. Her shoulders heaved as she used a towel to wipe the blood dripping from her nose.

Natsume, in the corner right in front of Nagamine, was also completely out of breath and had a nosebleed.

"Detective—" Miu drew closer and threw Natsume the towel she had used. "You've got it in you."

"You too—if you went pro, there's no mistaking you'd be a champion."

"And what's that worth, a women's boxing champ…"

"Does your mother know that you're boxing?"

"Of course not. She's the type who says women need to be ladylike. If she saw me like this she'd faint." Miu laughed, then exited the ring and went upstairs.

Natsume wiped his face with the towel, then got down from the ring as well. The manager and trainees were throwing questioning looks at him.

"Sorry for troubling you."

Jacket in hand, Natsume left the gym.

"What were you thinking?! She's a woman. Why didn't you go easy on her?"

"That would have been rude to someone who'd asked for a real match."

What did he mean—

"But now, I'm convinced."

With her hat low over her eyes, a pair of jeans, and a casual shirt, Miu walked into the train station at Mejiro. She took the Yamanote line and got off at Ikebukuro. Concealed amidst the surge of people, he and Natsume continued to follow Miu.

What in the world was Natsume thinking?

If they neglected to attend the investigation meeting, Yabusawa and the other chiefs would tell them off. Frustrated, Nagamine looked at his watch.

After passing through the JR gate, Miu entered a restroom in the station. Natsume stopped and watched intently.

After about ten minutes, she abruptly walked out. Pushing her way through the wave of people, she crossed the station compound.

"Kai—" Natsume called, to which a woman turned.

She looked fashionable, had long hair, and wore a skirt. As she gazed at him, her expression stiffened.

Studying the woman's face for his part, Nagamine was shocked. Although it was hard to tell immediately with her makeup, the person in front of him was, without a doubt upon close inspection, Miu. Even her chest seemed larger, as though she'd put on padding.

"I'd like to talk to you a bit more..." Natsume said, accosting her.

"At a police station, I presume?"

"Yes."

"I have two conditions."

"What would they be?"

"I'll talk to you. I don't want to talk to a person who wouldn't understand."

"And the other?"

"May I change? I can't relax looking like this. I have to dress up this way for my mom back home."

Nagamine watched Miu's face, and Natsume's back, from beside the interrogation room door.

He was a little irked that he'd been relegated to writing the report while the jurisdictional detective took charge of the questioning, but it was a promise to Miu and couldn't be helped.

"You're Kai, Ayano's lover, right?" Natsume began.

"What the hell?" Nagamine said, standing up.

"You be quiet for a bit, okay? I'll tell you everything. I've accepted it. I won't run or hide."

At Miu's words, he meekly sat back down. *You better tell us,* he thought as he glanced at her bosom, which was now flat.

"A chest binder?" Natsume asked her.

"Yes. I hate having breasts, so at work and at the gym, I wear one."

"Gender dysphoria," Natsume said.

Miu nodded. "You got it. I'm FTM."

When your body's sex is in disharmony with your conscious gender, you suffer from gender dysphoria, and FTM means being female in body but identifying as male, Miu explained.

"Way back from when I was still a kid, I had vague doubts about being a woman. I hated having long hair and wearing skirts, and the people I liked were always women. By the time I was in high school I was convinced that I was gender dysphoric, but couldn't tell anyone. Ever since I was little, my parents always wanted me, their only child, to be ladylike... But it became hopelessly difficult, and just when I was trying to confess to my parents, my dad died in an accident. My mom was horribly shocked and I couldn't worry her any more, so I ended up not being able to tell her I was gender dysphoric. For twenty-six years, I always felt alone."

"You met her one year ago."

"Yeah...when Ayano was being harassed by a weird man near my house and I tried to help her. But instead, I got beat up by Kamiya... Ayano brought me to her apartment and treated me. She was really concerned about the wounds on my face, so I told her it was a medal and laughed. And I confessed about the true me for the first time."

"Then you started dating her."

Miu nodded. "Even though I'd fessed up, I thought it wasn't meant to be, but unexpectedly, Ayano said she liked me. After that...I busted my ass to become a man who could protect Ayano. I trained my body, and mentally, I did my fucking best to become a guy she could always rely on. Because I loved Ayano.

Because it was the first time I had someone who was so dear to me. I thought Ayano also loved me in the same way. But I guess I was wrong…" Miu shrugged his shoulders with a lonely expression.

"That night, while doing roadwork, you saw Mr. Kaitani leave her condominium, is that right?"

"Yeah. I immediately went up to her room. I wanted to know why Kaitani had been in her condo. Then, when I looked around her room and found the condom, I tore into her. No wonder decent men ignored such a slut, I cursed her. Then Ayano got fired up too and said, 'Who're you to be blaming me?' Ayano came closer and exposed herself in her bathrobe and spat at me, 'Then satisfy me. Satisfy me completely. You can't even do that, so don't just blame me.' It was humiliating. That's the moment when my pride, which was always teetering, crumbled."

"That was when you pushed her onto the bed and strangled her."

"My mind went blank and I don't remember much… But I remember trying my damned best to choke back tears."

"Even from my viewpoint, I think you were pretty manly. That pride of yours set you apart from lowlifes who're violent toward women and cause them harm."

And what's that worth, a women's boxing champ—

What Miu had said at the gym came back to Nagamine as he listened to Natsume. Maybe what those words meant was that as a man, Miu didn't want to be hitting women.

"I'd loved for you to have upheld that pride," Natsume said.

"Right…" Miu hung his head. "May I ask something?"

"Go ahead."

"How did you…figure me out?"

"At first it was just a suspicion. When Detective Nagamine called you a 'tomboy,' you lost your temper. However, to me that seemed a little strange. A woman who moves heavy packages as her job, and who boxes, should be used to such comments and would have learned to ignore them. But your anger was disproportionate. A tomboy 'acts like a boy, even though she's a girl.' I thought perhaps the 'even though' bit ticked you off. Up until a little while ago I still wasn't confident, but I thought I'd ask your body."

"And…what did it tell you?"

"That gut punch was eloquent. I felt certain that your heart and soul were as unmistakably male as my own."

"I've gotta say, I had a bad feeling from the moment we sparred."

"In addition… If Ayano's lover turned out to be you, it made sense that she'd move to Ikebukuro despite the risk of encountering Mr. Kamiya. Your workplace and gym are both near Ikebukuro. She must have wanted to spend as much time with you as possible."

"Yeah…this past year was a special time in my life. If only I hadn't witnessed that," Miu sighed heavily.

"Did you take her cellphone because you'd be traced as a person she knew?"

"The texts would instantly tell you what sort of relationship we were in. I took it because I saw on TV or somewhere that even if they're deleted, the contents can be restored in the hands of the police."

Listening to Miu's response, Natsume nodded.

"Why 'Kai'?" Nagamine couldn't help asking.

Natsume glanced at him, then looked back at Miu and guessed, "Miu is a very feminine name. You must have thought that there'd be a disparity between even a nickname like Mii and the manly person you were trying to become. Mi-u…U-mi… *Umi* as in 'the sea'…whose alternative reading is *Kai*… You probably went through that thought process to come up with your masculine nickname…"

Miu's shoulders drooped, as though he'd been completely trounced. "Wow…"

"Apparently, she had said to acquaintances about you, 'He'd protect me with his life. He's the manliest person I've ever met.' At the same time, she said that although she loved you to death, perhaps it wasn't meant to be… There are many ways to protect your dear ones, I think. Was what happened the only possible conclusion for you two?"

Miu's eyes moistened heavily at the pointed question. It was clear that he was doing his damned best to choke back sobs.

"Let it go… Men cry, too."

Then wailing filled the interrogation room.

Day Off

What time are you coming home today?

It was as he left the company that the message came from Ryuta.

Atsuro Yoshizawa slowed his pace. Today, together with his subordinate Hattori, he had to entertain important clients. He would probably be out late.

"Let me send a reply real quick," he told Hattori, who was walking next to him, before typing on his phone, *I'll be late entertaining guests, so eat ahead of me. Your veggies too.*

Just a handful of seconds after he sent it, the reply came in three English letters: *YES.*

Rather curt—

"Your son?" Hattori asked, to which Yoshizawa nodded. "How old was he again?"

"Fourteen—second year of middle school."

"You must be close if you're texting each other."

"You think?"

"Around that age, don't they usually rebel?"

The rebellious age—for now, Ryuta wasn't showing any symptoms.

"Well, I guess my son is beyond that," Yoshizawa answered with some pride as they headed to the station.

That day's entertainment ended much earlier than he thought.

After parting ways with Hattori at Iidabashi station, Yoshizawa got on the subway.

He mixed in with the salaried workers heading home on the train just after ten o'clock. Holding on to a grab handle, he thought over the day's achievements.

The person he'd entertained that day was in charge of stocking a supermarket chain of over forty stores in the metropolitan area. Sounding out the client's opinion of the new snack that would be sold next month, Yoshizawa saw that it was going over well.

The reflection of his face in the window caught his eye. He looked tired. He would be. Since he'd been promoted to sales manager four months ago, he'd barely taken any time off.

I shouldn't be complaining, not in these times, he chided himself, drawing back a sigh.

He looked around the carriage. It wasn't just him. Most of the other passengers were also working their heads off for their families. For their families…

Hattori's words came back to him: *Around that age, don't they usually rebel?*

Ryuta wouldn't. He was a good kid who didn't cause his father trouble, perhaps partly because he'd lost his mother early.

Ryuta's mother Akiko had succumbed to breast cancer seven years ago, when the boy was in his first year of elementary school. He was alone often, so there had to be times when he felt lonely, but he never complained or whined to Yoshizawa. It seemed like Ryuta had come by some of his father's grit. He even had good grades, put energy into club activities, and did all of his chores.

But lately, Yoshizawa had noticed that they weren't conversing as much.

He'd always called home if he was going to be late at work while Ryuta was still in elementary school. They were just ten-minute conversations, tops, but he used to listen to his son go on about school and his friends. Then they switched to cellphones, and at some point, to texting.

He arrived at Oizumi Gakuen station before eleven. His condominium was about a ten-minute walk from there.

Lately, he'd been coming home past midnight more often than not and couldn't have real conversations with his son, but Ryuta might still be awake at that hour.

Yoshizawa walked homeward across the dim residential district at a brisk pace.

A white minivan idled at the park near his condominium. His march slowed when he saw someone getting out of the vehicle; he recognized the boy. Wasn't it was one of Ryuta's classmates—Jumpei Higuchi?

What could he be doing this late at night?

Yoshizawa thought of calling out to him, but when a second silhouette emerged from the car, he froze.

Ryuta? He gawked at the boy, who was wearing a sweatshirt and a backpack. There was no doubt. It was Ryuta—

A young man who'd come out from the driver's side and was saying something to Ryuta pulled some bills out of his wallet and handed them to him.

Ryuta took the money and walked off toward the condominium with Jumpei.

After the two boys' forms receded, Yoshizawa approached the minivan, slowly.

The young man who'd given Ryuta money was smoking a cigarette outside the car and cackling. There was another guy inside. They seemed to be twenty, give or take. Their tank tops left several tattoos exposed between them.

Passing by the minivan's side, Yoshizawa cast a glance through the open door as if he didn't really mean to. The interior was loaded with what looked like steel wire or bundles of cable.

The men might have been doing some sort of construction work, but why were they with Ryuta and Jumpei?

Part time work, he thought for a moment, but doubting that was the case, he dismissed the idea. There was no chance that they'd hire middle schoolers.

What *was* it?

He wanted to sprint right away to Ryuta and ask, but couldn't.

The look he'd just seen on his son's face was burned into his mind. The Ryuta who'd taken the money wore a dark, brooding expression that Yoshizawa had never seen on him until now.

Suddenly, he was walking faster. The path to his condominium seemed terribly long.

When he reached his unit, he struggled over whether to ring the bell or to unlock the door himself. In the end, he went for his keys.

"I'm home—"

When he opened the door, Ryuta was right near the entrance. Yoshizawa seemed to have caught his son as he was heading to his own room. Meeting Yoshizawa's eyes, Ryuta looked surprised for a moment.

"You're early..." he muttered, averting his eyes ever so slightly.

"Yeah..."

Yoshizawa wanted to question his son there and then, but his rehearsed words would not come out. Taking off his shoes and stepping up from the alcove, he pulled a snack from his briefcase.

"Our next new product... Wanna try it with me in the living room?"

"I'll pass for today. I have school tomorrow," Ryuta replied, his eyes turned away, and went into his room.

At a loss, Yoshizawa stood stock-still staring at the closed door.

The next morning, he woke up half an hour earlier than usual.

Hoping to bring the conversation around to it in the morning, he'd wound back the alarm by thirty minutes.

This shouldn't be too hard, should it? He just needed to say he'd seen his son the night before in the park. Just ask him: what connection did he have with those guys. It had to be something trivial. Despite the said guys' outward appearances, considering youth fashion nowadays, it didn't necessarily mean they were bad people. You even saw many musicians and athletes with tattoos on TV. He wasn't going to judge people by their appearances. There was no way Ryuta would associate with that kind of crowd in the first place—

He had ended up tossing and turning in bed until dawn thinking such thoughts.

Since he'd only dozed off for an hour, his head felt heavy, but he got up and left his bedroom. Ryuta wasn't in the living room. Always going out to school by the time his father woke up. Before, Yoshizawa would rise at the same hour and have breakfast together, but these days he was just too tired and slept right up to the last moment.

Usually, Ryuta would be having breakfast around now. Thinking he might still be asleep, Yoshizawa stepped toward his son's room, but saw that Ryuta's shoes were missing from the alcove. Maybe he'd left quietly so his father wouldn't notice.

Was he being considerate, or…

Thwarted, Yoshizawa took the newspaper from the letter slot and returned to the living room. He poured himself some coffee and sat on the sofa to skim the paper. An article in the corner of the local news section almost made him spit out his coffee.

Metal cables were disappearing from construction sites around the capital with alarming frequency.

It couldn't be… Uh-uh, not possible. What was he thinking? No way Ryuta was part of a gang of thieves.

He gave Ryuta money for food and allowances every day. He

made sure his son had enough.

But…could he be absolutely certain? How well did he really know Ryuta now?

Anxiety began to thrust up from deep in his heart.

For about the past month, he'd barely seen Ryuta. They hadn't talked, either. He didn't not even know what his son was doing with his time while his father was out of the house. Because they relied on texts, he didn't even know where Ryuta was messaging from.

Unable to contain himself any longer, he headed to Ryuta's room.

When he reached the door, however, he hesitated. Believing that trust was golden in a parent-child relationship, up until now he hadn't gone into his son's room without permission. But he couldn't afford that luxury at the moment. He wanted to hurry and find something to negate his anxiety.

He opened the door and entered. The first thing that came to his attention was the desk. Six crumpled five-thousand-yen bills were scattered over the top.

It was probably the cash Ryuta had taken from that guy yesterday.

Yoshizawa looked into the corner and his palpitations grew worse. A pair of blackened gloves and pliers lay on the sweatshirt Ryuta had worn the day before.

Yoshizawa left the office shortly after 6:30 p.m.

How long had it been since he'd wrapped up so early? He'd gotten into the habit of working overtime night after night even when he didn't have to entertain. Yet today, he hadn't been able to focus at all.

Given his state, there was no sense in him staying, and he had something to do as a father. He understood that, but he was scared of going straight home.

If he did and Ryuta wasn't there—well, he'd spend anxious hours alone, his imagination running wild. If Ryuta was home, on the other hand, he wasn't sure what to say to him face to face.

What a pitiful father.

Until now, he'd never been caught up in worries like these. He'd never even imagined being troubled by such matters when it came to his Ryuta. What was he going to do? He couldn't possibly consult anyone about this, either.

Suddenly, a certain man's face floated into his mind.

He would be able to dispense sound advice.

Though Yoshizawa didn't doubt that, he was also reluctant to contact the man, and not because he'd be laying bare his own pitifulness. The man was his one close friend to whom he could show his shabbiest worst. But these days, his friend was…

Yoshizawa looked at his cellphone and faltered.

As he drank his second draft beer, he heard the establishment's entrance swing open.

"It's been a while."

When Yoshizawa turned around, Nobuhito Natsume, who'd come into the pub, casually raised his hand.

"Boss, can I get a draft beer, a skewer assortment, a sashimi appetizer…and fried tofu and edamame," Natsume ordered from the chef at the counter before taking his seat at Yoshizawa's table. "Did I make you wait?" he asked with a smile.

"No, I'm just on my second glass. Sorry to borrow your time out of the blue like this…"

He'd called Natsume's cell after considerable hesitation. The man worked in twenty-four-hour shifts, so if he couldn't make the time, Yoshizawa was ready to give up. But Natsume had just completed one, and they'd arranged to meet at this familiar *izakaya*.

He was a close friend from high school back north in Aomori, and they'd both come to Tokyo after graduating. They'd continued to meet up while attending different colleges. Yoshizawa joined the confectionary company he still worked for right upon obtaining his bachelor's degree. Meanwhile, Natsume, who'd wanted to become a teacher since high school and who, Yoshizawa assumed, would continue on the path, instead enrolled in the graduate program in psychology and became a "judiciary technical officer," which involved interviewing offending youths at juvie and stuff.

Yoshizawa thought that Natsume, considering his experience with boys who'd committed crimes, might have solid advice about the matter at hand. At the same time, he was afraid to broach the subject. Natsume had switched jobs and was now a cop; his current occupation was precisely to catch anyone who'd run afoul of the law.

When Natsume's beer came, they toasted to start off.

"How's work?" asked Natsume.

"Ah… I made manager the other day, and I've been pretty busy…"

"Really? Congratulations."

"What about you?"

Natsume served with the East Ikebukuro precinct. Some time ago, when Yoshizawa had been drinking in Ikebukuro, he'd been bemused to witness a uniformed Natsume coping with a drunkard at a police box.

"I was assigned to the detective section," Natsume said. Yoshizawa thought his friend's eyes gave off a glint.

Yoshizawa couldn't quite manage to say congratulations, though Natsume must have wanted the job. "Is that right…"

"Is Ryuta doing fine?"

Yoshizawa started a little at his son abruptly being brought up, but nodded and replied with a choked "Yeah…"

"What grade was he again now?"

"Second year of middle school."

"Right...he was already that age," Natsume said wistfully.

Yoshizawa could guess what was on his friend's mind. Natsume's daughter Emi was the same age as Ryuta. When their kids were little, their families often visited each other, but that had come to an end ten years ago.

"Extracurriculars?" Natsume asked.

"He's in the kendo club."

"Just like his dad."

Yoshizawa had played kendo from elementary school to high school, and he was the one who had recommended the martial sport to Ryuta.

"About a year ago, he was in a competition. Maybe he took after me, it was a tight match that had my heart pounding quite a bit."

"Was it...'lose the battle to win the war'? Your national match was amazing too, wasn't it," Natsume reminisced, laughing.

Come to think of it, Natsume was in the boxing club during high school. He'd participated in the same nationals, so Yoshizawa had gone and watched. Although Natsume had such a gentle face, when he put his gloves on, he headed toward his opponent with a blazing competitive spirit that belied his everyday self, Yoshizawa recalled.

While their duels of choice differed, Natsume's fighting style was similar to his own. Maybe that was why Yoshizawa liked the man and continued to hang out with him.

His son faced opponents in the same daredevil manner as Yoshizawa, too, casting all caution to the wind. At the competition, Ryuta had gone all the way to the finals but had lost at the end. Dissatisfied with being the runner-up, he'd held back tears of frustration all the way home—every bit of which made Yoshizawa proud.

When Yoshizawa came back to himself, the table was lined

with several dishes. "You ordered a lot, didn't you?" he pointed out, appalled. "Don't ask for everything at once, it'll just get cold."

"We can talk more calmly like this." Natsume glanced at the employee who'd brought the dishes and was returning to the counter. "Usually we sit at the counter, don't we? Is this about Ryuta?"

Natsume must have figured that out when he'd entered the pub. As always, the guy had keen perception.

"Actually it is... I'm not sure if this is the type of thing I should be consulting you about, but...I don't have anyone else to turn to."

Yoshizawa recounted the events of the previous night—his son getting out of a white minivan and receiving money from a young fellow—and about reading the newspaper article in the morning and becoming sick with worry. "I can't imagine Ryuta has a hand in those cases, but try as I might, I can't stop worrying. I wanted to ask your objective opinion..."

Natsume just looked pensive even after Yoshizawa was done talking.

"It's weird, right?"

Natsume raised his face. "What is?"

"All I need to do is ask my son, you must be thinking. It might just be some misunderstanding."

"True... He might not answer truthfully even if you asked him, but I think talking to him first is important."

"I know. But I'm scared...that he might be getting his hands dirty with crime... The moment that comes out of my mouth, the trusting relationship that I've built with my son will crumble..."

"But you can't leave this alone, can you?"

Yoshizawa shook his head.

"Tomorrow... I'm off duty. Would you like to come investigate with me?"

"When you say investigate..."

"I don't like what I'll be doing, but it's not like I don't understand where you're coming from as a father. So how about we investigate Ryuta's behavior for a day...and think of what to do afterwards?"

The next day, he had an important sales meeting—

But this was no time to be thinking of such things. Ryuta was far more important.

"All right," Yoshizawa nodded.

The next morning, when Yoshizawa heard Ryuta's door open, he headed to the front entrance.

"Morning," he called out.

Ryuta, who was putting on his shoes, turned around in surprise. "Morning..." he mumbled back. He held his school bag in one hand and was wearing a backpack.

"Today, I'm coming home a little late."

"Got it..." Ryuta answered curtly and left.

Yoshizawa immediately started the day's preparations. First, he called the office and used a sick day to take time off. The subordinate who took his call was flustered. The key meeting wouldn't amount to anything without the manager.

Hanging up, he caught a glimpse of the portrait of Akiko on the living room cupboard.

His wife, who usually looked like she was smiling, seemed to be rebuking him today. What did Akiko think of him—a father who couldn't fully trust his own son?

After ten, Yoshizawa also left and headed to the shopping street by the station. At a men's attire counter in a large supermarket, he bought new clothes and a new hat. They'd naturally have to shadow Ryuta to investigate his behavior. Yoshizawa chose clothing that would make him as difficult to recognize as possible and paid the bill still wearing his fresh getup.

As he was waiting at a roundabout by the station entrance, a car honked. He turned around to a parked, black sedan. Its window descended, and Natsume stuck his face out of it. Yoshizawa got into the passenger's seat.

"How was it?" Natsume asked as soon as Yoshizawa got into the car.

"Ryuta went to school as usual."

"When will he be out?"

"Today he has six periods, so after three o'clock. Even later, if he has his club."

Yoshizawa looked at his watch. It was only past eleven.

The day before, asking Natsume when to meet up, he'd wavered. Since his son was in school until three, Yoshizawa could at least attend his meeting, leave early, and still make it. Ryuta, however, might use some excuse to get out of school early as well, so they'd arranged to meet at this time.

"Have you eaten?" asked Natsume.

"Nope."

"Then let's buy food somewhere before we go to the middle school."

Natsume drove the car out. On the way, they stopped at a convenience store, where Yoshizawa bought a rice ball and a sandwich for his lunch. He had it in the car after they drew up near the middle school's gate. They chatted about old times for a while. After a few hours of being stuck in a car seat, though, Yoshizawa found it intolerable. Meanwhile, he didn't see any sign of discomfort on Natsume's face.

"Do cops do this sort of thing every day?" Yoshizawa asked.

"It's not like you shadow or stake out people all the time, but you do spend an entire night monitoring a suspect on occasion."

"Isn't it difficult?"

"Your body learns to do it."

"Not that. Suspecting people as your job."

Natsume looked at him intently.

Yoshizawa thought it even now. The policing profession didn't suit Natsume. Having known the man for years, he sincerely felt that doubting people had to be the most difficult thing for Natsume.

But Natsume choosing such an occupation also made painful sense to him as a fellow father.

Ten years ago, there had been a case involving a serial assailant in Nerima Ward. Natsume's daughter, one of the victims, had been hit in the head with a hammer and left in critical condition, comatose.

Several days after the incident, Natsume had gone in front of television cameras as the victim's family in order to appeal to the culprit.

Stop this, hurry and turn yourself in.

As though to ridicule his tearful plea, another case occurred and resulted in the girl's death.

If the culprit had turned himself in or been apprehended back then, Natsume probably wouldn't have chosen to become a police officer.

Wasn't Natsume spending his days now mired in hatred? There had to be a more soothing path for him than the hard life of a detective who confronted criminals day in, day out. As his close friend, it hurt to watch Natsume be this way.

"It's certainly true that my current job is to suspect people. People lie. Even more so, when they've committed crimes. My job is to catch such people," Natsume replied unflinchingly.

His clear gaze was just the same as in the old days; had he, then, traded in his heart instead?

"Suspecting people, suspecting my son like this, is too much for me. Even if it means turning a blind eye, I want to keep believing..."

They heard the sound of the bell and turned to the school. It was the bell signaling the end of the school day. After a while, students started pouring out of the gate one after another. The two men watched intently.

Ryuta came out. He was walking with Jumpei.

"It's Ryuta!"

"With the blue backpack?"

"Yup."

"And the one who's walking with him is..."

"His friend Jumpei Higuchi."

Ryuta and Jumpei had been friends since elementary. Yoshizawa remembered how the boy used to come to their house to play. It seemed that both of Jumpei's parents worked and that he was often home alone. The two kids still frequently visited each other as far as Yoshizawa knew.

Natsume drove out slowly. The boys got on a bus at a stop near the middle school.

Where were they going?

About fifteen minutes later, the two got off the bus. Walking together again, they entered a park. After some time, they came out wearing sweatshirts and jeans; they must have changed in the public bathrooms. Once more they plodded along.

They entered a family restaurant along the main road. The place had a small parking lot, but to avoid being noticed, Natsume parked slightly further back along the road. From there they could see the building, though not what the two boys who'd gone in were up to.

After ten minutes or so of waiting, Yoshizawa saw a familiar white minivan drive into the restaurant's parking lot. "That white minivan..."

"Is it the one you saw that night?"

There were many similar vans, but there was no doubt, as it was those same men who entered the restaurant shortly after.

What the hell were Ryuta and his friend doing here? What in the world could they be discussing with those men? Yoshizawa had a bad feeling about it, and just sitting there doing nothing was unbearable.

"Should I try going in?" Natsume said, likely sensing Yoshizawa's agitation. "If I sat near them, they wouldn't notice, and I might be able to overhear their conversation."

"I'm counting on you..." Yoshizawa said and nodded.

Just then, Ryuta emerged. Running diagonally across the pedestrian scramble, he went into a convenience store across from the restaurant. After some time, Jumpei and the two men also came out but headed to the parking lot in the back. Ryuta popped out of the convenience store soon enough, a shopping bag in one hand, though it wasn't clear what he'd purchased. He made a call at a public phone, hung up, and stood at the pavement in front of the convenience store.

It looked like he was waiting for the white minivan to come around from the parking lot.

Yoshizawa's desire to believe in Ryuta did battle in him with the urge to dash out of the car and drag his son home.

He took out his cellphone and placed a call to Ryuta, visible on the other side of the crosswalk.

"Yes..." came the blunt greeting.

"Hi, it's your dad..."

The reply wasn't immediate. "Why are you calling so early?"

"Where are you right now?"

"Near school."

Yoshizawa took in Ryuta's lie, careful not to rush this. "I'm going to finish work early today. You wanna eat out somewhere?"

"I have plans right now..."

The white van slid out of the parking lot. Natsume pulled out and followed behind.

"What plans?" Yoshizawa asked Ryuta as they approached

him.

"Doesn't matter. You have your business dinners and I've got my own!" he snapped and abruptly hung up.

The minivan ahead of them forced a right turn precariously close to oncoming traffic and stopped next to Ryuta. Natsume had trouble doing the same against a stream of vehicles.

Yoshizawa tried calling one more time, but Ryuta's phone must have been turned off and he couldn't get through. He could only watch, dumbfounded, as the minivan his son had gotten into sped away.

At last, the right turn signal lit and their sedan lurched forward, but even after driving for some time, they couldn't find the minivan.

"Sorry…" Natsume apologized.

"It's not your fault. Besides…"

It might be better this way—or at least, half of him thought so.

The words he'd just heard Ryuta utter lingered in his ears. It was the first time his son had snapped at him, and it rattled him.

Yoshizawa was afraid of witnessing Ryuta's next actions, to be honest.

"What do you want to do? Should we wait for him to come home?" Natsume asked gingerly.

"I have a favor to ask you… I want to visit Emi."

Thinking over why he'd suddenly thought of her, Yoshizawa began to hate himself. Was the idea of a family in greater misery than his own so consoling to him? He was a terrible person.

"Yes…Emi is in a hospital in Itabashi. We'll still be able to make the visiting hours."

"Oh…ah…actually…"

"Would you please do it? Emi would be happy too." Natsume glanced at him and flashed a smiled that pierced Yoshizawa's heart. "But first, there's somewhere we need to drop by."

It was at the convenience store Ryuta had gone into earlier that Natsume stopped the car. Pulling the sedan up into the parking lot, Natsume got out of the driver's seat, and Yoshizawa followed after him.

Instead of going into the store, Natsume approached the public phone out front and stared at it, muttering, "I wonder who he called."

"I've no idea…"

Let alone whom Ryuta had called, Yoshizawa felt like he no longer knew his son.

Natsume knocked and opened the door to the hospital room. "Come on in," he ushered Yoshizawa.

Natsume's wife, Minayo, who was sitting at the bedside, stood up with a surprised look on her face.

"Mr. Yoshizawa, it's been a while," she greeted with a smile.

He occasionally met with Natsume, but when it came to Minayo, it had truly been a while. How long, he couldn't remember exactly, but the image of her sorrowful face after that incident had stayed in his mind. Reuniting with her like this, he was relieved that she'd regained at least some of her cheerfulness.

"I'll go buy some juice or something," Minayo said, placing the illustrated book in her hand on her daughter's bed before stepping out.

"She's gotten big, hasn't she?"

Yoshizawa couldn't really bring himself to face her, but at Natsume's words he directed his gaze at Emi, who lay asleep on the bed. She had indeed grown. She'd been so little when he used to see her before the tragedy.

It was as if he were being confronted with the weight of—ten years.

It was a cruel sight, too.

A tube was stuck in Emi's nose. She had lived on that bed,

unable to eat by herself, unable to speak, unable to move, for ten years. Natsume and Minayo had continuously watched her in that state, for ten years.

It was monumentally sorrowful to lose someone dear to you. Yoshizawa knew how it felt, having lost his beloved wife. Yet, the sorrow of someone passing away did heal, if only slowly. The months and years turned the deceased into a beautiful memory.

For this couple though, the scene before their eyes was the brute reality. They would need to keep accepting such a reality as long as Emi lived.

"Uncle Yoshizawa is here. Do you remember him? He used to play with you a lot," Natsume tenderly spoke into her ear, touching her hand.

Emi's hand twitched in response.

"She moved just now," Yoshizawa said, surprised.

"Yes...because she's alive. Many people seem to conflate being in a vegetative state with brain death, but actually it's completely different. The brainstem, which controls autonomic nervous activity like breathing and pupil response, is still active in a vegetative state, so you can breathe on your own and sometimes even respond to being called. Also, you regain consciousness in rare cases. A few years ago, there was a news story from overseas about a man who woke up after being in this state for nineteen years. Though the chances are extremely slim..."

Yoshizawa looked at Emi. She indeed was breathing by herself, and her eyelids were twitching.

"Hold her hand, if you don't mind."

Yoshizawa slowly approached the bed. When he touched Emi's hand, he felt her weakly gripping back.

"Hey, Yoshizawa—"

Yoshizawa looked at his friend.

"Believing isn't about what your eyes see at a given moment."

Natsume's words seized and shook him.

No matter how things stand now, have faith in what the future will bring. Isn't that what his friend was trying to tell him?

"You're right..."

The man really believed it. Though he couldn't communicate with her or see her smile now, he believed that someday, no matter how slim the chance, his daughter would recover.

What about himself? Had he really believed in Ryuta? Wasn't he, as a father, merely scared of being betrayed by what his eyes could see at a given moment, of that which he held dear? Had he only been using the word "believe" to run away?

"Natsume... I'm going home. I'm going to wait for Ryuta to come home. Then I'll talk to him upfront. Even if he's an accomplice to a crime, I won't stop believing in his future. I'll show him that he can get back on his feet, no matter what."

"Go for it. Just like with your kendo styles, clash head-on even if you'll both end up bruised," Natsume said with a smile and big nod.

The detective offered to drive him home, but Yoshizawa declined. The only time his friend spent with his family was probably his days off duty.

As Yoshizawa walked down the hallway with Natsume, who at least wanted to see him off to the exit, the phone in his pocket vibrated. The call was from a number he didn't recognize. "Give me a moment," he excused himself and took out his cell.

When the caller introduced himself, his heart churned.

They headed to Kiyose Police Station in Natsume's car. As soon as it pulled up to the building, Yoshizawa raced to the front desk.

"I received a call just now... I'm Ryuta Yoshizawa's father."

"Please wait for a moment at that bench," he was told by the receptionist. He sat down, waiting for the detective who'd contacted him to arrive.

So I was right...

According to the detective, the police had found and caught Ryuta, Jumpei, and the two men as they were stealing cables from a construction site in Kiyose.

As he hung his head at the bench, Natsume, who'd parked the car at a nearby meter, came in and sat next to him. Still hanging his head, Yoshizawa said, "If I only had the courage day before yesterday, when I came across that scene, it might not have come to this."

"By the time you noticed, he was already an accomplice, wasn't he?"

"That's true… I wonder why Ryuta did it. I have no clue. What the hell was he unhappy about? After Akiko passed away, I tried so hard in my own way, for his sake…"

After some time, a middle-aged man in a suit came to them. "I'm Sugimoto from the detective section… Which one of you is Ryuta's father?"

"I am." Yoshizawa stood up from the bench.

"And this is?" Sugimoto indicated Natsume with his hand.

"My friend…"

"I see… Would you come up with me alone."

"Certainly."

As he was about to follow behind Sugimoto, Natsume called out to stop him and handed him a piece of paper folded in half. When Yoshizawa opened it, a five-digit number was written on it.

"What is this?"

"A puzzle you need to solve."

He had no idea what Natsume was talking about. Now wasn't the time to be fiddling with puzzles.

Yoshizawa stuck the piece of paper in his pocket and went up the stairs. When he entered the room labeled "Detective Section," he saw his son sitting at one of many desks. When their eyes met, Ryuta sulkily turned away.

He could think calmly about the future conversing with Natsume in the hospital room; now, seeing Ryuta with that expression, irritation overtook him.

Why had he gone and done this? Where was the Ryuta he knew?

"He hasn't spoken since we apprehended him. We had no choice but to look up your number on his cell and contact you."

Yoshizawa walked over to Ryuta, and with all his strength, slapped him on the cheek.

"Why did you do it?! I believed in you."

Holding his cheek, Ryuta glared at Yoshizawa and said, "For...no real reason."

"What?!"

Yoshizawa stood Ryuta up by his collar.

"Sir, please calm down," Sugimoto interceded, but Yoshizawa didn't loosen his grip.

He wanted to believe in Ryuta's future like Natsume had told him to. But in order to do that, he had to be as stern as necessary and get his son back on his feet.

"What's with that attitude? You don't think getting caught like this by the police is an embarrassment to your father and mother?! When did you change?!"

"You don't know anything..." Ryuta spat, dropping his gaze.

A puzzle you need to solve—Natsume's words suddenly came to mind.

The meaning of those numbers... He'd seen them somewhere. But where? He hauled in his memories, all the while staring at Ryuta's lonely expression.

The public phone outside the convenience store. The serial number on the public phone—

No way...

Yoshizawa let go of Ryuta's collar and turned to look at Sugimoto. "How were Ryuta and his friends caught?"

"It was thanks to a tip. The caller said he knew someone was going to steal cables at a construction site in Kiyose around 7 p.m."

"Did that call come from a public phone with this serial number?" Yoshizawa pulled the piece of paper from his pocket.

"I'd need to look into it..."

"Isn't that it? You're the one who tipped them off," Yoshizawa said, looking at his son.

"Why...would you..." Ryuta stammered.

"I was watching you the whole time. What you guys were getting up to today."

"Give me a break!"

Ryuta gave Yoshizawa a fierce shove.

"Give me a break, why now?! After ignoring me forever? You didn't care what happened to me! You always went on about believing me, but really all you wanted was to not deal. I'm not that strong, okay? Why wouldn't you watch me *all* the time? Why didn't you stop me sooner?!"

Shouting and crying, Ryuta struck Yoshizawa's chest.

The words, one by one, pierced him with an almost physical pain. Yoshizawa could only absorb his son's words as best he could.

When he went down the stairs sapped of his strength, Natsume was waiting at the reception bench.

"How did it go?" he stood up and asked.

Yoshizawa handed him the scrap of paper with the numbers. "You're keen as hell."

"I just wondered why he'd use a public phone when he had his cell on him."

"Even his own father didn't think of that."

"*Because* you're his father, you couldn't stay calm under those circumstances," Natsume consoled him.

But was that really true?

He hadn't been properly watching Ryuta. He'd been forced to realize that he hadn't been facing Ryuta. As fearless as they were during kendo matches, in real life they were both cowards. It was the first time he'd seen his son show such raw emotion. Crying and shouting, Ryuta had spilled his guts.

The whole thing had started quite casually.

Apparently, while he and Jumpei were playing at a gaming arcade, those men had accosted them. If they had the time, did they care to make 2,500 yen an hour at a job?

Realizing that the job was to commit theft, the boys tried to refuse the next time they were invited but were too scared of the men. They'd gotten trapped deeper and deeper as a result, but they'd actually wanted nothing more than to quit.

Ryuta must have been waiting for his father to notice his odd behavior. Yet, Yoshizawa completely failed to intercept the SOS signal that he was sending out: the five-thousand-yen bills scattered on a desk in an unlocked room, a set of pliers large enough to cut chain on conspicuous display. And he was forced, as a last resort, to inform on himself.

Yoshizawa had not been properly watching Ryuta—had not even been bothering to wake up half an hour early to chat with his son. Just as Ryuta accused, Yoshizawa had used the word "believe" cheaply, as a sanctuary.

"I'm a failure as a father..." he muttered.

"Did it hurt, what he said?"

"Yeah...it did," he replied with his hand on his chest, his eyes looking into Natsume's.

"Me, I envy you. Yours can come at you like that. So now..."

"Yup...we'll try to start over," he announced to Natsume.

"Today was a worthwhile day off for both of us. Thanks."

"What are you saying? I'm the one who should be thanking you."

"You believe in Ryuta's future."

"Yeah. Of course."

"I bet Ryuta believes in you, too. I rarely get to witness such wonderful moments these days. Back to work from tomorrow..."

With that, Natsume turned and walked away.

Yoshizawa spent some time watching his friend's back, which looked just a bit forlorn.

Rice Omelet

Keiko Maeda motionlessly stared at the death portrait. Hideaki was beaming from within the black frame. His white teeth flashed against his tanned skin in a smile. Keiko loved this photo the most.

Three days ago, the apartment they lived in had caught on fire at nighttime, and Hideaki, who had been asleep, had been engulfed in the flames.

When it happened, Keiko had been on a partial night shift at a nearby hospital, and just when it was about to end, Hideaki had been carried in as an emergency patient. He had massive burns all over his body and was already taking his dying breaths when he entered the treatment room on a stretcher. When Keiko saw his body, entirely discolored a dark red, she almost stopped breathing.

Since the injuries were extremely severe, she was choosing not to show the body to visitors at the overnight vigil.

Looking at Hideaki's death portrait revived many memories that had lain in her heart. It was about two years old, from that time she'd first introduced him to Yuma. Hideaki had taken her and her son to an amusement park in a minivan.

No doubt, Hideaki must have been nervous about meeting Yuma. Even so, smiling like his life depended on it, he did his best to become quick friends with her son. Yuma, who was incredibly shy, must have sensed Keiko's hardships raising him as a single mother; he, too, acted his cheerful best with the stranger that his mom had introduced to him.

The picture had been taken as the three of them were eating the *bento* lunches that she'd packed. At the time, everyone had been smiling.

Having offered incense to the deceased, the head nurse Morita came to Keiko's side.

"Ms. Maeda, this must be very difficult for you. Don't you worry about work, take as many days off as you have to until you feel better," she said, gently touching Keiko's shoulder.

"Thank you."

"Yuma, please look after your mother."

"Yes."

Yuma, who'd answered in a flat voice, seemed oddly aloof, as though he'd abandoned himself to following the ritual without any drama. When her previous husband Koichi had passed away in a car accident, he'd clung to her waist and sobbed throughout the funeral service.

Perhaps Hideaki's passing hadn't affected Yuma at all.

Although they never made it official, for Keiko, Hideaki had been her husband without a doubt. Yuma, however, might have seen him as nothing but a freeloader. Having lived with the two for the past couple of years, Keiko knew.

After Morita stood up and left, Keiko noticed Yuma looking at her, but when their eyes met, her son quickly averted his.

Though it was just one moment, Yuma's gaze caught in her heart. His profile still betrayed no emotion, but she'd felt something piercing in that gaze.

She wanted to attend to his feelings but had no idea what he was thinking now.

Keiko turned her gaze from Yuma back to the altar.

Most of the guests at the funeral were from the hospital she worked at. Not only her own family and relatives, but Hideaki's parents, too, were no shows at today's vigil. She'd looked up his parents' contact info and notified them of his death, but their response had been chilly. She didn't know the details, but Hideaki seemed to be a prodigal son who'd caused a considerable amount of trouble for his relatives.

For that reason, although they were not formally husband and wife, Keiko had taken it upon herself to arrange for the funeral as the chief mourner.

A man she didn't recognize was offering incense. As she stared at him wondering who in the world he might be, the incense finished burning, and he approached her himself.

"Mr. Hideaki Sato's family, I presume?" the kindly, slim-faced man asked her. "I am deeply sorry for your loss. I'm Natsume from the East Ikebukuro precinct."

He'd politely expressed his condolences before offering her his card. It certainly did say that he was Nobuhito Natsume from the East Ikebukuro precinct.

Learning his identity, Keiko felt less on guard than thrown off balance. This tall, slender man clad in a black suit was distinctly not her idea of a detective.

For her, the word summoned someone with drilling eyes tinged with distrust; yet, the man she beheld had nothing oppressive about him. His tidy hair, not in the least greasy, and his thoughtful pupils reminded her more of the young doctors and technicians she knew than any detective. A lab coat would have become him, more so than his suit.

"I am in charge of the arson case," he cut to the chase in the gentlest voice.

"I see…"

Over the last two months, the neighborhood in Zoshigaya, Toshima Ward where Keiko's apartment was located had suffered successive arson cases, in each of which garbage dumps and parking lots had been doused with gasoline. Her apartment fire had occurred amidst the spree.

"What's happening with the investigation?"

"We're certainly on it. We're not sure yet if this arson was committed by the same perpetrator, but for the sake of the victim and the bereaved, we'll do everything in our power."

As he said this, Natsume turned toward Yuma, who was standing next to her, a gaze that was kindly, enveloping. Her son, who'd been expressionless until now, looked back at the detective, startled. Keiko felt like she understood part of the reason.

Natsume's demeanor was somehow reminiscent of Koichi, who'd been an X-ray technician.

"We have something called a victims' consultation room at the station. Please don't hesitate to drop by if there's anything."

Natsume's compassionate gaze won Keiko over, but at the same time, a strange sense of unease seeped out of some gap in her heart.

"Please...catch the culprit soon." Averting her eyes somewhat, she uttered the words that the bereaved were expected to in face of a detective.

When she looked at the clock, it was past seven thirty.

"Yu, wake up."

Keiko knocked on the door. Her friend was still asleep in the adjacent room, so she couldn't be loud.

Going back to the kitchen, she poured whisked eggs into the frying pan. Once they were moderately firm, she added the chicken rice she'd cooked in advance. Wanting a spatula to adjust the shape, she rummaged through the shelves below the sink but couldn't find one. This wasn't her own kitchen, after all. She gave up and used chopsticks for the final touch; then, she packed the rice omelet into the lunch box.

After their apartment had burned down, Keiko had been given a place to stay by a friend of hers, a former high school classmate who was now the "Mama" at a club in Ikebukuro. They hadn't kept in touch after graduating but had united in the past year when the friend came down with appendicitis and found herself in Keiko's hospital.

Though never very close during their high school years, Keiko had taken care of her even outside of work hours, seeing that her former classmate was single and particularly inconvenienced by her admittance. She must have felt obliged; when she got wind of the tragedy, she offered one of her apartment's three bedrooms for an extended stay saying that it wasn't in use. Keiko had taken advantage of her kindness and moved in with Yuma, but planned on finding a new place to rent within the week.

She wanted to shake off what had happened and start a new life with Yuma, the sooner the better.

She heard the front door clamp shut, and when she went into the hallway, Yuma's shoes were gone from the entrance area. Keiko hastily grabbed the lunch box and ran after him.

Yuma wore a helmet in addition to his school uniform and was heading toward the bike racks.

He went to school on a scooter. He'd earned his license this past summer vacation, having turned sixteen, and bought his ride with the money he'd saved from his part-time job.

"Yu, your lunch."

Her son turned around sluggishly.

When she handed the box to him, he took it as though it were a chore and stuck it into his bag. He straddled the scooter and turned the key without saying a word. Even with his helmet on, she could tell that his face was expressionless.

Keiko's heart ached as she watched him race away on his scooter.

At some point, Yuma had turned into a kid who didn't let out his emotions.

Once upon a time, he'd been affectionate and considerate. When Koichi had an accident and passed away, Yuma was in his second year of elementary school. Keiko suffered the depths of despair, but her son, while no doubt equally devastated at losing his father, cheered her on with a bright smile.

At an age when kids were most consumed with play, Yuma instead helped Keiko, tired from working odd hours as a nurse, with the housework. No matter how spent she felt when she came home, just seeing Yuma's smile gladdened her. As long as she had him by her side, she needed nothing else.

She would live only for Yuma from now on. She'd honestly thought that until two years ago, when she met Hideaki.

A bike accident that had fractured both his legs landed him in Keiko's hospital.

Apparently he'd been a reckless youth, joining a biker gang and what not, but was an honest truck driver at that point.

At first, she didn't see him as a member of the opposite sex. He was just a patient, and a rather bratty one. Keiko, thirty-seven then, was eight years older than him, so that was part of it. In addition, Hideaki was the diametric opposite of all the men she'd known until then.

In his hospital room, Hideaki often used dumbbells to work on his upper body. Both his immobile legs steadily lost their muscle, but his chest and upper arms grew until they seemed ready to burst.

She'd thought nothing of seeing her patients naked, but now found herself unable to look away as the sweat dripped off Hideaki's chest onto his toned abdominal muscles.

For his part, he might have noticed the attention.

As Keiko came into his room one day when he was soon to be discharged, Hideaki forced a kiss. Then he started rubbing her breasts, hungrily, from over her white uniform.

She couldn't resist his daring overture.

It was as though a gust of wind had blown off a bolt she'd desperately been holding down as a woman ever since Koichi's passing. She could only wonder where all the moisture had been in her parched body as the lustrous flow streamed out of her unchecked.

When he was discharged, Hideaki asked her out on a date. They went into a hotel and made love the very same day. For the first time in a while, clinging to Hideaki, her body scaled into pleasure. No, not for the first time in a while—this joy, she'd felt for the first time in her life.

Never had she experienced such intense pleasure, not with any of her past dates—no, not even with her dear departed Koichi.

She felt her body was melting from the heat of Hideaki's thrusts. Her mind was going blank, white on white. But every time, just when her pleasure was about to crest, Yuma's image flickered in her mind.

Her son mattered more than anything to her, no matter how many times she was loved, and however much her body craved it—she at least retained enough sense to think so.

From then, she came to meet with Hideaki at a hotel once a week, but didn't seek anything beyond that. She also hadn't told Hideaki about Yuma.

Keiko believed that even if she joined her body with Hideaki's for a fleeting moment, she would unfailingly go home to Yuma as his mother.

After some time, Hideaki unexpectedly proposed to her that they start living together, with the understanding that they'd eventually get hitched.

While ecstatic over his words, Keiko was worried. She had Yuma—

After agonizing over it, she told Hideaki the truth. She had a son in middle school. She made the confession prepared for a break-up, but Hideaki started asking her to introduce him to Yuma.

Although Keiko couldn't tell if Hideaki really meant it, the three of them got into a car Hideaki had arranged for and went out to an amusement park, where she watched Hideaki interacting with her son with ease. With this man, Keiko thought, she and Yuma might win happiness.

Some days later, she told Yuma that she wanted to live with Hideaki and marry him in due course.

Yuma, however, was revolted by the idea. No one was his father except Koichi, and he just couldn't trust Hideaki, he said.

Keiko didn't think that Hideaki was untrustworthy, but she understood why her son might reject her taking a new husband.

Even as she concluded that her only choice was to persuade Yuma over time, Hideaki cancelled his lease and pushed his way into their home.

She couldn't turn him away. In any case, if they lived together for a while, Yuma might come to see Hideaki in a better light. She attempted to bring her son around with that hope in mind, and he reluctantly consented.

But after living together for some time, Hideaki turned into a different person.

It started with him quitting his trucker job. He said he was fired for slugging a manager with whom he'd never gotten along.

From then on, making no effort to be reemployed, Hideaki adopted a new lifestyle: sleeping during the day, going out to *pachinko* gambling parlors, and drinking out at night.

He came up with one excuse after another to ask Keiko for money. Neither Yuma's college fund nor Koichi's insurance payout was off limits for him. By the time she knew, her actual savings were nearly drained, too.

Whenever she complained and stood up to him, he became violent toward Keiko and Yuma. He was especially ruthless with Yuma, who'd never come to see Hideaki as his father. Keiko, no match for the man physically, could only watch.

She considered driving Hideaki out of her home but didn't follow through. If she did such a thing, she might lose him altogether.

Yuma was dear to her, but she didn't want to give up Hideaki.

Hideaki was just acting out over being fired; once he regained his senses, he'd go back to being the winning man who took them to amusement parks.

She wished that in her heart, but Hideaki's behavior failed to improve.

Ever since he'd barged into their home, the trust that had cemented Keiko and Yuma's relationship had vanished, and a deep ditch stretched between them.

There was Yuma's face from that one time that clung to her mind even now.

As she was having sex with Hideaki in their room, Yuma had come home and obliviously opened the sliding door. Beholding the scene froze him in place, and he stood stock-still. Although Keiko immediately tried to uncouple and cover herself with a blanket, Hideaki wouldn't let her. Tightly gripping Keiko's waist, he kept thrusting into her from behind.

"Stop…" Keiko pleaded, but Hideaki wouldn't even then.

Yuma's eyes were filled with disgust.

"Hey, ya feeling good?! —Hurry and become a man who can please women like this."

Keiko just couldn't shake off Hideaki, who continued to jerk his hips, laughing. In fact, Yuma's contemptuous gaze, and a sense of shame that transcended words, entwined with her man's thrusting, had transported her to untold heights of ecstasy.

Perhaps she had stopped being a mother then—

The conflagration must have been her divine punishment. Henceforth, she was dedicating her life to making amends with Yuma.

Hideaki's funeral was over, and Keiko intended to go back to work that very day. She was on the late shift, which started at noon. She still had time.

Exiting the condominium, she decided to visit her apartment before going to the hospital. The day before, she'd reached out to her superintendent, according to whom the police were done with their inspection. She could now go inside.

The site where Hideaki had been caught in flames. It certainly frightened Keiko, but another her urged that, like it or not, she needed to stand there once again if she were ever to embark on a new life.

Taking the street that ran by the Sunshine 60 skyscraper from East Ikebukuro, she headed to the Zoshigaya apartments. The Ikebukuro General Hospital where she worked was along the way. From there, the apartment was less than a ten-minute walk.

It came into sight as she proceeded through the residential district. Pain gripped at her heart, and her legs faltered. Even so, she needed to see the disastrous scene in there with her own eyes, she told herself, and forced her legs onwards.

The two-story wooden apartment building had eight units total. Although it had avoided burning down entirely, there were no signs of anyone living there now. The unit they'd lived in, #101, was at the corner on the first floor.

A scorched odor assailed her nostrils the moment she opened the door. When she entered, the kitchen just past the shoe alcove didn't look all that badly burnt, but the floor was soaked with a tremendous amount of water. Still wearing her shoes, Keiko stepped up from the entrance area and slowly looked around the kitchen. While the furnishings might not have turned to ash, they were too black with soot to serve any use again. To begin with, she wouldn't want to live surrounded by stuff that had sat where Hideaki died.

Keiko examined the sink. A plate of rice omelet that she'd

cooked for dinner that day was still there. Yuma and Hideaki usually finished all her dishes, but oddly some of it had been left over.

The sight awakened bitter thoughts in her, so she turned her eyes toward the Japanese-style room behind the kitchen.

The room had burned down almost entirely. She took a firm step onto the charred floor mats and entered it.

A stack of paper on the veranda outside had been set on fire, and Hideaki had been caught in the flames as he slept in this room.

Keiko quietly closed her eyes and put her hands together.

"Good afternoon—"

Hearing the voice, she snapped back to reality and looked toward the entrance. Right outside the front door, which she'd left open, bowed a man.

It was the detective, Natsume, whom she'd met at the vigil. Why was he here?

"Would it be okay if I came in?" he asked in a reserved tone.

"Go ahead," Keiko answered.

Natsume stepped into the alcove but looked at his feet and seemed to hesitate a little.

"Please, as you are."

"In that case," he said with a light bow and entered the kitchen with his shoes on.

"Earlier, too, I came here to inspect the site. It's in a terrible state."

Keiko turned toward him across the dining table. "Yes…"

"How are you faring? Is your current residence…" he asked, choosing his words carefully.

"A friend has taken us in and we're okay for now… But we need to find a new place to live asap."

"With most of your things wrecked, it must be very difficult."

"As you can see, we had a simple life. I don't care about what happened to our furniture. A person's life, though, won't come back."

"That's true..." Natsume agreed. "I heard you were there during his final moments."

"Yes, because he was brought to the hospital I work at."

"There's something I need to ask you... What exactly was your relationship with him?"

Keiko couldn't blame Natsume for wondering. "He was my husband. We just hadn't formalized it yet, it was a common law relationship."

"I see."

"My son is still at a sensitive age, so I wanted to deal with that after things settled down."

"Then Hideaki was an adoptive father for your son. He must be quite shocked by what happened."

That wasn't true, Keiko thought, but she replied, "Yes..."

"At least, his wife was with him when he passed away."

Keiko's eyes welled up with unfeigned tears at Natsume's words.

"Are you the chef in your family?" the detective changed the topic as though to lighten the mood.

"Yes."

"It can't be easy when you work, too."

"I just make easy meals."

"A rice omelet that day," Natsume said looking at the sink. "Usually kids love that."

"It's Yuma's...my son's favorite, so I always cook it when I can't make up my mind," she answered, and finding all this funny, couldn't stifle a laugh.

Natsume gave her a blank look.

"No, it's just that seeing you, I can't believe you're a detective... You're too different from my image of one."

"What kind of image is that?"

"A scary person who's kind of stern and has a piercing gaze."

"Many are like that. I haven't been one for long, so it might just be that I don't give off the proper vibes yet."

That was surprising. Although his fresh bearing made him appear young, Keiko had assumed that they were about the same age.

"I switched jobs," Natsume said, picking up on her puzzlement.

"Switched… What were you before?" she couldn't help but ask.

"Do you know what a judiciary technical officer is? I worked at a juvenile detention center for kids who had committed crimes. I evaluated their psychology, et cetera. I was thirty when I joined the force."

Hearing this, she understood why Natsume's eyes, seemingly so kind, had made her nervous.

The detective before her had dealt with many offenders in the past and peered into their hearts. She absolutely couldn't show this man a chink in her armor—

The goodwill she'd held for Natsume vanished in an instant.

"Yesterday, I visited the hospital, but it seemed you hadn't come back to work yet, so I was planning to visit again after this. Meeting you here was good timing. There are a number of things I need to ask you."

Keiko braced herself, hoping Natsume didn't notice. "What might they be?"

"Was Hideaki taking anything like sleeping medications?"

"Sleeping medications?"

"Yes, the forensics autopsy detected traces of sleeping medications in his remains."

"He might have taken mine. I keep irregular hours and it's hard for me to sleep, so I got a prescription. I stored it in that cupboard drawer, but sometimes there would be less…"

"Then he might have not been able to sleep that day and taken your medication. How unfortunate. He might have noticed the fire earlier if he hadn't taken any."

"If I'd properly kept track of my medication, Hideaki…"

"I may have said something ignorant. It's not your fault that he passed away. It's the fault of the culprit who started the fire." Natsume's gaze seemed to sharpen from the anger he felt toward the perp.

"You're right… Excuse me, but I need to go to work soon…" Increasingly discomfited by Natsume's presence, Keiko looked at her watch.

"Yes, I almost forgot, I need to return this to you." He took something out of his pocket and gave it to Keiko. It was an evidence bag containing a cellphone that seemed to have warped from the heat. "Hideaki's. We kept it for a bit."

"I see."

"It seems he'd promised to meet with someone that day. The night before, he had sent a text message. It was to a woman named Shizuka Okamoto. Do you know her?"

"I don't."

It was a lie. Shizuka Okamoto worked at a hostess club in Ikebukuro, and Hideaki had become an ardent fan of hers. He'd spent liberally there several times a week, using either the money Koichi had left her or the savings she'd worked so hard for. Then, after closing time, he'd gone to hotels to hold that woman in his arms until morning.

Keiko had pressed him about his relationship with Shizuka many times, but Hideaki would spout that he could do as he pleased since they weren't married. Then, complaining that he'd sacrificed his old life to marry her and be with them, he'd turn the tables on her and blame her for failing to persuade Yuma to let them marry.

Hearing him say so always made her feel that Hideaki was

sincere about getting married, at least. If he did stray, if he did raise his hand against them, it was simply due to his frustration over not having tied the knot yet.

What a vicious circle. If only he'd continued being the kind man that he'd been toward her, Yuma might have come to trust him, too, in time.

Then it wouldn't have come to this—

She couldn't stand having Hideaki stolen from her.

"Mind telling me where you live now?" Natsume requested, handing her a memo pad.

Keiko shut out all of her feelings and wrote out her friend's address.

"Are you sure you're fine?" Morita, the head nurse, called out to her as she entered the nurse station.

"Yes, sorry for worrying you. I'm fine now."

"Well, don't push yourself too hard."

Like Morita, most of her coworkers offered her words of condolence and encouragement.

During her shift, she tried her best not to think about the case. She couldn't let it slow her down. From now on, just like in the past, she and Yuma were going to weather life together. She wanted to work hard at her job and save up money to send him to a good college.

Since meeting Hideaki, she hadn't been a good mother. No, she'd been the worst of mothers. From now on, more than anything, she would treasure her life with her son. From now on, she would devote all of her life to making him happy. She intended to be reborn.

Yet, a dark shadow slipped into her chest as soon as she recalled Natsume's antics.

According to Morita and the others, the detective had come to the hospital the day before asking many questions about Keiko and her family.

Perhaps Natsume didn't believe the case was the handiwork of the serial arsonist.

When she looked at the clock, it was almost time for her to replace the IV drip for the patient in Room 312. Keiko left the nurse station, prepared the drip, and headed onward. The private Room 312 was at the very end of the hallway, beyond which lay the emergency stairs.

When she entered, Yoshio Yasuoka smiled at her from his bed and said, "Are you okay now?"

Faced with his gentle smile, she relaxed a little, but he seemed to have lost some weight while she'd been away. Yasuoka, the director of an accounting office in Ikebukuro, had been admitted two months ago with an ailing stomach.

No matter how tired from work or how vexed she'd been by Hideaki's selfishness, nursing Yasuoka had been her oasis. Gentle, considerate, he was the opposite of Hideaki.

Widowed by his spouse and lacking children, he had to be lonely in his hospital room. He seemed to have gradually come to hold special feelings for Keiko, who attended to him every day.

Especially after seeing a bruise that Hideaki had left on her, he'd grown sincerely concerned about her wellbeing and lent her a sympathetic ear.

After I'm discharged, why don't you break up with Hideaki and marry me, I'll take good care of you and your son.

She'd been elated to hear him say that. Why couldn't she have come across a man like him before running into Hideaki? But regret as she might, it was already too late.

"That reminds me, yesterday a detective visited me."

Her hand, which had been inserting the needle for the drip, froze. "You?"

"Yes… The police seem to think that the apartment caught fire around ten past midnight. They heard that you hadn't been at the nursing station at the time and came to talk to me."

"What was the detective like?"

"Tall, young… I think he said his name was Natsume."

Hearing that, Keiko fell into a gloom.

"There isn't anything for you to worry about," Yasuoka said, sensing her anguish. "I told them that you were giving me my drip the whole time. We heard the sirens and wondered if it was a fire."

Keiko looked at Yasuoka's thinning arms and at the numerous needle marks. Her heart ached to think of it. She'd been such a burden—but it was all over now. She wanted to think it was.

She inserted the drip needle into a vein.

"As usual, it doesn't hurt when you do it," Yasuoka smiled.

It was already totally dark when her shift ended and she left the hospital.

She needed to hurry home and make Yuma dinner. Crossing through the parking lot with brisk steps, she pondered what to put on the menu.

Tired as she was from getting back to work, today she'd cook an elaborate meal for Yuma. Her body seemed to shake off some of its fatigue at the idea.

The door opened on a car parked in front of her, and someone stepped out.

"Good evening."

The exhaustion that had lifted just a moment ago came swooping back when she saw who it was that had greeted her. "Do you have some business with me?" she returned brusquely.

"I apologize for inconveniencing you, but I wanted to ask if I could talk to Yuma a little."

She showily looked at her watch. "It's already nine o'clock."

"Just a little. I could have gone straight to him, but I thought it might be better if his mother were present."

Even if she refused now, there was no mistaking that he'd eventually seek out Yuma. In that case, it would be better, indeed, if she were there too. Keiko reluctantly agreed and got into the passenger's seat of Natsume's car.

The road to the condo felt interminable.

"What kind of kid is Yuma?" Natsume spoke out of the blue.

"What kind… He's that difficult age, but I think he's a good son. You're asking his mother, though."

"No, when I met him at the vigil, I thought he was a tough kid, too. I mean, he's had to bear losing his father, and now his adoptive father."

"He's been through a lot of hardship. Even though Hideaki wasn't legally his father, I think my son feels shaken in his own way…" Keiko told the detective, implying that he should go easy on Yuma.

"I will exercise discretion."

Her friend was still out working, so Keiko had Natsume ask his questions in the living room.

"Sorry to impose on you at this late hour. I just wanted to ask you some things regarding the night of the fire," Natsume began, facing Yuma, who sat on the sofa.

Keiko, who was sitting side by side with her son, studied her son's profile. Yuma seemed to be nervous and had his eyes cast down as he listened to Natsume.

"That night, did you have a fight with Hideaki? The next-door neighbor heard voices like someone was arguing," Natsume inquired in a calm, deliberate manner, looking straight at Yuma.

"Not really… When I got home, I had an argument with him about nothing. Like always."

Natsume showed no impatience at Yuma's muttered and vague reply.

Seeing Natsume confront her son, Keiko remembered that

the detective had once worked at a juvenile detention center. The man was used to talking to boys like Yuma who were at an impressionable age. Never domineering, he seemed to excel at unspooling his interviewee's mind.

"Yuma, you left the house after that, right? Do you remember around what time?"

"Ten thirty or so…"

Why had Natsume quit his previous job and become a detective? The point elicited her interest and suspicion, but she wasn't about to ask. She could do without becoming better acquainted with a cop.

"Where were you until you came home?"

"Around… I rode my scooter. I ran out of gas, so I went to a gas station and ate a hamburger and then rode around again."

Natsume smiled when Yuma said this. "Of course, you're young, you have a big appetite."

Yuma raised his face with a puzzled expression.

"You'd already had rice omelet for dinner, right?"

"I didn't eat it…"

"I see." Natsume nodded, then continued, "So you got on your bike for a while and came home. Do you remember around what time?"

"I think it was past 1 a.m. I was surprised because there were a lot of fire trucks and ambulances parked around."

"You intended to come home after your mom did, is that right?"

Yuma nodded. "Because I didn't want to come home to just him…"

"In that case, you weren't anywhere near the apartment at twelve o'clock. That's too bad. I wanted to ask if you there were any suspicious persons around at that hour."

"Dunno…" Yuma shook his head.

After that, Natsume asked Yuma which gasoline station he'd

stopped at and wrote it down in a memo pad.

Keiko was anxious over just how much of Yuma's story Natsume believed. Her son had been riding his scooter around twelve o'clock, at the time of the fire. He didn't have a proper alibi.

"Thank you."

When Natsume made to stand up from the sofa, Yuma said, forcefully for the first time, "You don't think our fire was part of the serial arson case, do you?"

"The police need to account for many possibilities as we conduct an investigation. Although questioning you, the victim's family, like this, even as you're grieving over the loss of your adoptive father, pains me."

"I'm not really grieving. I'm relieved that he died," Yuma threw out with a defiant look at Natsume.

Keiko was alarmed by her son's words. Why go out of his way to say that?

"Thank you, sorry for my rudeness."

Staring at the door Natsume had shut, Keiko hesitated for a moment. Then she put on her shoes and flew out of the apartment. She called out to stop Natsume, who was standing in front of the elevator.

"Please don't make too much of what Yuma just said," she tried to justify her son's behavior to the detective. "He might not have liked Hideaki much, but my son is definitely not the kind of child who would do such a thing."

"He was at least half serious, though. I already knew they didn't have a good relationship. One of his friends said that Yuma grew to hate Hideaki for getting violent with both of you."

Keiko winced. So he hadn't just made inquiries at the hospital but also gone to Yuma's school.

"But I don't think hatred necessarily leads to murderous intent, either."

Natsume bobbed his head and got onto the elevator that had arrived.

Inspecting the apartment's restored white walls, Keiko asked the accompanying real estate agent: "How much is the rent?"

"Including the admin fee, it's 108,000 yen."

That was more than double their previous apartment's rate, but a two-bedroom property in Ikebukuro no doubt cost that much even if it wasn't very spacious.

When she asked, "Yu, how do you like it," he assented with a silent nod.

He had to be tired from visiting properties since the morning. Despite her son's lukewarm response, Keiko took a liking to the apartment. It wasn't too far from Yuma's school, and with two rooms, he'd have his own study.

She was far over her planned budget but resigned herself to working harder at her job.

"I'll sign the contract," she told the agent, and indulged herself with glances around the interior. Picturing the life that she could start with Yuma here, she felt thrilled for the first time in a while.

After they returned to the real estate company to pay the deposit, she and Yuma walked back to the condominium.

She realized that it had been a while since she'd spent time with Yuma. He walked a pace ahead of her in silence. Her son no longer initiated conversations with her, and Keiko, herself, had no idea how to these days. Yuma had been a talkative kid once. As soon as Keiko came home from work, he'd go on about whatever had happened at school like he couldn't wait.

After Hideaki joined them, Yuma became a different person. She'd hurt him badly enough that he was now a different person. Slowly, though, she was going to mend their relationship. They were moving into a new apartment and starting a new life, redoing this one step at a time.

She stopped in front of the supermarket.

"Yu—" she called out, to which her son slowly turned around. "What do you want to have for dinner today?"

Yuma thought for a while. "A rice omelet, I guess?"

The hint of sorrow in her son's eyes gave her pause.

Although she wanted to eat with Yuma, Keiko had a late shift again that night. Once she made and wrapped the rice omelet, she went to work.

It was almost nine o'clock, according to her watch. There had been no emergency cases that day, and peace reigned in the nurse station. Just when she thought it would be nice if it stayed that way until the end of her shift, Natsume strode in.

The expression on his face filled her with dread.

"I would prefer you didn't come to my workplace. If you need to speak with me, come to my house," she requested firmly, glancing at her coworkers.

"I'm very sorry, but there was no time for that… Yuma came to the police this evening."

"To the police?"

"He confessed to setting the apartment on fire," whispered Natsume.

She couldn't process what he was saying. What a bad joke. But Natsume's earnest gaze dispelled that possibility.

What in the world was going on—

"Is there somewhere we can speak?" Natsume insisted, and they headed to the lobby.

"What's going on?!" she demanded.

"Please calm down," the detective tried to appease her. No one was in the lobby at the moment, but he was still speaking in a near whisper.

"Around six o'clock tonight, Yuma came to our police station.

He said he wanted to tell me something. When I listened to him in a room, he said he had lit the apartment on fire."

"There's no way that could have happened."

Why would Yuma say such a thing? She couldn't make any sense of it.

"There is nothing to contradict his confession right now. It's been verified that he did drop by a gas station at around 10:00 p.m. that day, but the staffer also testified that Yuma had come and filled his whole tank up the day before as well."

Keiko's heart started to hammer when she heard this. The previous day too?

"Riding his scooter enough to use up a full tank in a day is hard to imagine, and I found it strange. He turned himself in as I was wondering about that. Apparently, that night, Hideaki came home just as Yuma was about to have dinner. They got into an argument, and your son was struck in the head several times. He rushed out of the house. The episode seems to have honed the hatred he'd felt toward Hideaki into a murderous impulse. Using the refueling pump on the veranda, he transferred the gasoline from his scooter into plastic bottles, went back to the gas station to refuel, and bided his time, riding his scooter around again, until Hideaki went to bed..."

"But... Yuma really said that?" she asked in disbelief.

Natsume nodded. "Would you come with me to the station? I'll be waiting in the parking lot." He gently placed his hand on Keiko's shoulder, then left.

It was unbelievable—

Why would Yuma make such a confession? He certainly wasn't the culprit.

The only possibility that came to mind was that he was protecting her. Keiko felt a tight pain in her chest at the conclusion.

Was Yuma actually trying to take the fall for a mother like herself?

Even standing up was a challenge, but Keiko hurried to Room 312.

"What's wrong?" Yasuoka asked, beside himself, sensing a crisis from Keiko's expression alone.

"Apparently Yuma confessed to the police."

"What?!" let out Yasuoka, stunned.

Keiko couldn't stop her body from shaking. The more she thought about Yuma, the worse her shaking became.

"Why would he..."

"To protect me. I can't think of any other reason."

Yasuoka turned a pained look at her.

"Sorry... I can't do this anymore..."

Yasuoka covered his eyes, taking her meaning, but immediately lifted his face and nodded. "I understand. You don't need to worry about me. I'll always be waiting for you."

His smile skewered her heart. Consumed by guilt, she couldn't bear to look at him. She had used a good man like Yasuoka.

She said sorry one more time and rushed out of the room.

Using the emergency stairs right by it, she scrambled down to the first floor. The stairs connected to the outside and were a shortcut to the parking lot.

Natsume, who was standing by the car, noticed and looked at her.

"There's something I want to talk to you about," Keiko announced as she faced him.

During her whole time in the passenger seat as they headed to the police station, Natsume remained silent.

Anticipating the questions he would be asking her soon, Keiko turned over in her head the answers she might give him.

She was prepared for grim days to come. Even so, she wanted some inkling of hope for her life ahead to persist...

After he saw the bruise Hideaki had left on her, Yasuoka became her sounding board. *She should leave a man like that.* Keiko was vaguely aware that Yasuoka felt affection towards her. Then, one day, he proposed to her, asking her to marry him after his discharge. He would then devote his remaining life to taking good care of Keiko and Yuma.

If I can be with you, I'll do anything—Yasuoka's words made something pop in Keiko.

His offer could be her last chance at happiness.

She told him it would be difficult for her to ditch Hideaki, among other things. That if she suddenly talked about breaking up, she didn't know what he would do to her. Then, when she casually told him that if only Hideaki would die, they could be together, Yasuoka repeated his vow with a blank expression: "I'll do anything to be with you."

With that confirmation, Keiko made up her mind.

There had been a string of arson cases in her neighborhood lately. She could use that, she suggested to Yasuoka. The hardest part was the alibi, but he promised to provide one for her.

That day, right before midnight, Yasuoka made a nurse call to Keiko indicating that he was feeling ill. After bringing an IV drip into the room, she quickly changed into regular clothes that she had stored in the locker.

"I'm okay here," Yasuoka told her, and she exited through the emergency stairs directly outside of the room. Then she ran home. At a run, it didn't take more than five minutes from the hospital to her apartment.

Once she was finally there, she headed to the side with the veranda. The light in the room was off. Plastic bottles she'd filled with gasoline were on the veranda. She'd taken it from Yuma's scooter in the morning while he was asleep. She splashed the fuel on bundles of paper and the outside wall of the apartment. Peeping in through a gap in the curtains, she ascertained that the figure wrapped in blankets was fast asleep.

Then, with a shaking hand, she lit the match.

How had she been able to do that? Just remembering the sensation of lighting the match made her tremble at her own cold-bloodedness.

She'd just wanted to become happy. To escape from such a life.

Keiko looked at her fingertips. They were shaking slightly.

"You slipped Hideaki the sleeping medication that we detected in him, didn't you?" Natsume, sitting across from her, said. In the back, there was another desk where another detective was writing something on paper.

Keiko nodded.

She'd wanted him to be sound asleep and to die without too much suffering, at least.

"Weren't you afraid that Yuma would be home?"

"He hated being alone with that man and went out whenever he was there. Just as you said, I thought he wouldn't come home until I did."

Natsume, who had been staring at Keiko, nodded slightly.

"Detective, did you guess from the outset that our fire wasn't part of the spree?"

"I wasn't confident. But it seemed out of place because the fires up until then had been in places like parking lots and garbage dumps where no one would be placed in direct danger. So I investigated the victim, and indeed there seemed to be issues with Hideaki's behavior. You had an alibi that you were working at the hospital, and when I heard that during the time of the fire you were in Mr. Yasuoka's room, I went to visit him."

"I bet he was such a bad liar, you started to think I might be the culprit."

"He wasn't such a bad liar, actually. But when I asked if you were always the one who put in his IV drip, he answered that he asked for you when you were available because you were good at it. When I took a glance at his needle marks, there were several that were obviously far from his veins. Beyond being good or bad, I thought it wasn't the work of a nurse. He was desperate—about covering for you."

There was the sound of a knock and a detective came into the interrogation room. He whispered into Natsume's ear. Natsume breathed a small sigh and returned his gaze to her.

"Another detective has been questioning Mr. Yasuoka, and your stories appear to be consistent."

"It was something I asked him to do unreasonably, and he pitied Yuma and me. Please, he should receive as light of a punishment as possible."

"Whatever the case, imprisoning Mr. Yasuoka might be difficult." A cold sensation ran down Keiko's back as Natsume's gaze sharpened. "He hasn't been informed, but he has terminal cancer and his remaining days are numbered. You, knowing that, just used Mr. Yasuoka."

Maybe Natsume had seen through almost all of her. Looking into his eyes filled her with so much dread that she hung her head.

She'd been elated to hear him say, *After I'm discharged, why don't you break up with Hideaki and marry me, I'll take good care of you and your son.* She'd wondered, *Why couldn't I have come across a man like him before running into Hideaki?*

But she had already met Hideaki. It was too late.

The pleasure of rough sex with him was something she'd never be able to forget. It was like a drug. Her body knew she would never be satisfied with any other man.

"Why did you try to kill him?" she heard Natsume's voice ask.

"It was both love and hate…"

"Love and hate?"

"Since we first started living together, that man wouldn't even work. He took the money my previous spouse left us, as well as my own savings, to play around. When he was cross about something, he resorted to violence towards me and Yuma... In that sense, I hated him, but at the same time, I loved him more than anyone else could. I didn't want to lose him. If he was going to be stolen by another woman anyway, I might as well kill him with my own hands..."

"Stolen by another woman... Indeed, it appears as though Hideaki meant to marry Shizuka Okamoto."

She felt an intense shock at Natsume's words and raised her face in disbelief.

"He must have been planning to leave you as soon as you ran out of money. He'd have left you one day, on his own. But that isn't what I was asking you. Why did you try to kill him? Tell me your real motive."

Natsume was staring at her with sorrowful eyes.

"I don't understand what you mean. I just told you my motive—"

"Do you know why Yuma turned himself in?" interrupted Natsume.

"It...was to protect me, wasn't it?"

"Is that what you think?"

What other reason could there be?

There was a long silence. Natsume shook his head slightly and directed the other detective not to include the next part in the transcript.

"Yuma wanted to be arrested so that he would be sent to a reform school or a juvenile detention center. He couldn't live with you anymore."

"Wh-What do you mean..." Keiko asked, perplexed.

"You saw the text message Hideaki sent Shizuka, didn't you.

Having read it, you were sure he would be with Shizuka—and away from home. Am I wrong?"

Natsume's words gouged her heart. They dug into its recesses, to its dark depths.

"But Hideaki, feeling ill, came home."

Feeling ill—so that was why some of it had been left over.

"What are you… I don't understand what you're trying to say at all," Keiko maintained desperately.

"The one you tried to kill wasn't Hideaki, but Yuma."

Natsume's words ran her heart clean through.

"Don't screw with me!" she shrieked.

Confronted with the truth she'd been trying so hard to scrub from her mind, she felt like she was going insane.

She just wanted to be happy. To escape from such a life. She'd thought a second marriage, with Hideaki, would change everything. Weighing Yuma and Hideaki against each other, training her eyes on what happiness truly meant to her, she learned that a grotesque demon dwelled in her heart.

"How…how did you…" she somehow squeezed out the words.

"The rice omelet."

"The rice omelet?" she parroted.

"Apparently, Hideaki had said time and again to Shizuka, 'I don't feel any attraction towards that woman, but she knows how to cook.' And so, according to her, he always ate the dinner you made when he was home. There was only one rice omelet, the leftover one by the sink. Hideaki's stomach contained very little food."

"So what?!"

"If you were sure he'd be home, wouldn't you have made two of them?"

Keiko stared at Natsume and bit her lips.

"For his last supper, you made Yuma his favorite dish."

She almost nodded along but stopped herself in the nick of time.

She couldn't admit to it. If she admitted to *that* here, she would no longer…

"The person I killed was Hideaki. I will atone for that crime from now on, in prison," she somehow pulled herself together and declared.

"A lot of people seem to confuse going to prison with atoning for a crime, but the two aren't the same. The defense will likely request extenuating circumstances for your near-daily violent treatment at Hideaki's hands, and many of your fellow citizens will even sympathize with you. Is that what you seek, first and foremost?"

Natsume was facing her with an unrelenting look.

"What do you mean?"

"There is no evidence for what I just said. The facts of your crime are that you started an apartment fire and killed Hideaki. But Yuma caught on to it. That night, when he left the house on his scooter, he noticed that the gasoline he'd filled his tank with the day before had been extracted. When he saw that his apartment was on fire, he knew that you were the culprit. And that the one you really meant to kill was him—"

Yuma had caught on.

She desperately held back her brimming tears.

"You killed two people. You took Hideaki's life and murdered Yuma's heart. You did something atrocious, below even a fiend. Until you accept that, you don't have the right to use a word like 'atone'—nor can you ever face your son again."

Unable to bear meeting Natsume's eyes, Keiko lowered her gaze.

"No matter what happens, Hideaki won't come back to life. Yuma's heart, on the other hand—maybe it can live again. But in order for that to happen, you need to confess to the real crime you committed. You need to spend the rest of your life staring down the ugly, cold-blooded heart that was beating inside of you. You'll have to bear your son's hatred, and society's, henceforth. If you don't go down that path of thorns, you can't possibly atone for what you did to Yuma."

Natsume's words weighed heavily on her. She'd committed a terrible sin that was here to stay.

Natsume directed the detective behind him to resume taking notes.

"Who did you try to kill?"

Keiko raised her head. The man, his eyes strong, was staring at her.

"M-My son…"

The moment she answered, tears came flooding out, and she couldn't see the man anymore.

When she closed her eyes, she saw Yuma. He was gazing at her with lonely eyes.

Wondering if she'd meet him again someday, she kept her own shut awhile.

Scar

Kumiko Tanabe arrived at Ikebukuro East High School well before one o'clock.

When she looked into the staff room, most of the teachers were finishing lunch and chatting while drinking tea.

Kumiko entered the staff room and looked for a sign of Machida. The homeroom teacher for the Junior C class, Machida was sitting at his own desk. He was looking through a textbook to make preparations for the afternoon lesson.

"Mr. Machida, looks like you're hard at work," Kumiko called out to him.

Machida looked up from the textbook. "Ah, Ms. Tanabe, you too."

"Is Miss Nakamura at school today?" Kumiko asked about what had been on her mind.

"Nakamura… Oh, now that you mention, she wasn't here today either."

He said it as though it were someone else's problem.

He was an unreliable homeroom teacher. She felt frustrated about the man before her, but more than that, disappointment in Yuka overcame her.

"Is that right…" Kumiko muttered and left the staff room. She entered the counseling room two doors down and let out a loud sigh.

Yuka Nakamura hadn't come to school today, either—

The day before, when Kumiko had gone to talk to Yuka at

her house, she'd said she'd do her best to be at school the next day.

Yuka was a high school junior who repeatedly refused to come to school. Even more troubling was her compulsion to hurt herself. She had countless scars from cutting into her left arm with a knife. No matter how many times they talked face to face, Kumiko couldn't determine the exact reason for Yuka's truancy and wrist-cutting.

Day after day, out of all the students who came in for counseling, Yuka was the one to whom Kumiko paid the most attention.

She pulled out her cellphone and texted, *Yuka, what happened today? Call me back please.*

When it was past 5 p.m., Kumiko started on her work report.

That day, two people had come in for counseling. One was a senior who had concerns about his path after high school. The other, a guardian, had a sophomore girl who was always partying out lately.

Kumiko's cellphone chimed. It was a text from Yuka.

I'm suffering. I don't know what to do anymore. Maybe I should never have been born.

The message, more pressing than usual, put Kumiko on edge.

She called this time, but the ringtone sounded idly on and Yuka wouldn't pick up at all.

Kumiko put the unfinished work report in her bag and left the counseling room. As she walked down the hallway, she tried calling Yuka's mother.

Kumiko intended to visit Yuka's home, but it was likely that Yuka's mother was out working. If the girl didn't come to unlock the door, Kumiko wouldn't be able to get in. She didn't want to worry Yuka's mother more than necessary but thought it would be best to contact her, in case they were dealing with the worst-case scenario.

When Kumiko shared the situation over the phone, Yuka's mother said she would try her best to leave work as soon as possible and head home.

Kumiko also hurried toward Ikebukuro station and headed to Hibarigaoka, where Yuka's home was located.

When she got off onto the platform, she found Yuka's mother among the sea of people getting off the train. It seemed they had been on the same one. Yuka's mother was a canvasser for an insurance company in Nerima.

"Excuse me!" Kumiko called to her, to which the mother turned around.

"Ah, Ms. Tanabe. I'm very sorry you've had to come to Hibarigaoka so many times. She seemed fine when she left home this morning… Why in the world…" the mother muttered in bewilderment.

"At any rate, let's hurry and get to your place."

They got into a taxi outside the station and headed to the Nakamura residence.

In about five minutes, they reached the condominium. Kumiko had the mother open the door, and they went into the unit. Going through the entrance, Yuka's room was immediately to the left. Kumiko knocked on the door.

"Yuka, it's me… Are you there? If you're in there, answer."

"Leave me alone!" Yuka's shout came from inside the room.

It was a shout that seemed to reject everything whatsoever, but just hearing it, Kumiko was a bit relieved. Yuka was alive.

"Yuka, calm down. Let's talk a little. May I open the door?" Kumiko asked in a gentle tone.

"No! Don't come in! It's all my fault! It doesn't matter what happens to me anymore!"

She sounded quite hysterical. What could have happened?

Ms. Tanabe—I'll try. I won't run, and I'll try, Yuka had said, with a smile even, when they'd talked the day before.

"Yuka…just show me your face. If you don't want to talk, I won't make you. Can I open it?"

"No!"

Kumiko slowly turned the knob and opened the door.

Inside, it was pitch black. Keiko heard muffled sobs. From the light that leaked in from the hallway, she could tell Yuka was on the bed along the wall.

"Yuka…I'm going to turn the lights on, okay?"

Kumiko reached for the switch. She started the moment she saw Yuka in the light.

The girl's left hand was stained red. It wasn't just her hand. The sheet was colored with an immense amount of blood. A box cutter lay on the bed.

"Yuka!" Kumiko rushed to her, immediately took her hand, and inspected the wound. The cut looked quite deep. Wrapping the girl's wrist with a handkerchief, the counselor turned and called out, "Please, call an ambulance!"

"Ms. Tanabe…what should I do?" Yuka's mother muttered with a weak look on the way back from the hospital. "I just don't know what to do anymore…"

Yuka's wound hadn't been life-threatening, but her hysterical state hadn't subsided. She seemed better off being admitted to the hospital until she calmed down, and had been left there in that state.

Seeing the mother's haggard face, Kumiko thought the doctor who'd decided that it would be best to admit Yuka had made the right call for the mother as well. Yuka's mother needed to work in order to make a living, and she was at the limits of her fatigue, Kumiko sensed.

"She used to be such a cheerful child…"

The mother's mutter gave way to sobs.

What could have caused the girl to suffer to this extent?

Scar

Kumiko had been counseling Yuka for nearly a year and a half but still wasn't sure why. She felt utterly powerless.

Kumiko had come to know the two after Yuka's mother had been led to the counseling room by her daughter's homeroom teacher a year and a half ago. Yuka had recently started to skip school and to stay out late, and her mother needed advice.

From her story, Kumiko easily fathomed the cause of Yuka's truancy. Not long before, Yuka's father had been arrested by the police. He had been working at a construction company until he was charged with bribery over the development of a building lot. As a result Yuka's parents got divorced, and her father was serving time in prison. Kumiko was certain that it must have cast a dark shadow over the girl's heart.

From then on, Kumiko had counseled her. Yuka had steadily regained her spirits and started coming to school again, but then relapsed about a year ago. Moreover, she began to make incisions in her arms and wrists with a box cutter.

Why, after she'd almost recovered—

Her truancy aside, Kumiko wanted to at least stop her cutting and continued counseling her, but it hadn't produced any promising signs so far.

It wasn't that Kumiko had no clue what might be driving Yuka's self-harm. A short time before Yuka had started cutting, she'd been involved in an ordeal. But was that really the cause?

Not feeling quite satisfied, Kumiko felt lost over how to proceed.

"Vice principal, this is serious—" an admin person came into the staff room and said in a loud voice while Kumiko was talking to Machida about Yuka.

Wondering what was happening, she turned toward the staffer, who headed toward the VP's desk and started talking to him. At the word "police," there was a commotion among the teachers around Kumiko.

"What business could the police have?" Machida uttered in his seat in front of her.

She could only tilt her head in puzzlement. "Who knows?"

The staffer left the VP's side and exited the room for a moment. It seemed the police were in the hallway outside.

With everyone's eyes on him, the staffer urged, "Please, come in," and a man in a suit entered.

When Kumiko saw the man, she was shocked. Nobuhito Natsume—

Still in disbelief, she looked at him for some time, but it was him without a doubt.

She couldn't take her eyes off of Natsume as he headed to the vice principal's desk. For his part, the man seemed to have noticed Kumiko as well, to judge from the slightly surprised look on his face.

Natsume showed the vice principal a police badge and started talking about something. Then, he and the vice principal left the room together.

Kumiko watched Natsume's back in a daze.

When she left the lounge to return to the counseling room, the door to the principal's office opened, and out came Natsume. He bowed to the principal and vice principal and then started walking toward the front entrance.

She couldn't help but follow after him.

"Natsume!" she called out from behind.

He stopped and turned around.

"So you were working here." Smiling, Natsume walked back toward her.

When was the last time—

The last time they'd seen each other might have been after they all finished graduate school and went out drinking. That was almost fifteen years ago.

His trim figure, his clean ungreasy hair, and those gentle eyes which seemed to engulf a person whole—Natsume seemed not to have changed much. Only the police badge he'd flashed earlier was at odds with her past impression of him.

"Why…" Kumiko murmured.

"There was a case near here yesterday, and I came to ask about it."

"It's not that! Why do you have a police badge?" she pressed, quite seriously.

Natsume laughed. "It's not fake. I'm on the police force these days."

"You quit being a judiciary technical officer?"

Natsume nodded.

Even so, she couldn't believe *that* Natsume had become a cop. What was going on? "Why…"

"It's a long story. I have work to do, and I need to get back to the station as soon as possible."

"To investigate the case you just mentioned?"

"Right."

"Is it connected to my school?" she asked, concerned.

"To be honest, I'm not sure if there's a connection or not. Yesterday, around noon, a man was found dead of unnatural causes in a condo in South Ikebukuro. We canvassed for eyewitnesses in the vicinity, and a girl wearing this school's uniform had been seen near the condos. So I was a little curious…"

"Are you saying that a student at this school is connected to the case?"

"No, I'm not sure about that yet. Maybe she was just passing through. Even then, she may have witnessed the culprit, so I at least want to hear what she has to say. I wanted to know which students hadn't been at school yesterday around that time."

She seemed fine when she left home this morning—

Keiko recalled what Yuka's mother had said and felt a sinking sensation in her chest.

"I have to go. Sometime soon, let's all go out drinking again," Natsume said, then raised his hand and headed to the exit.

While they'd been in the same entering class at the same university, Kumiko hadn't met Natsume until they were both in the graduate program. Their departments had differed: Natsume had studied educational psychology in the school of education, Kumiko social psychology in the school of arts.

They became fast friends, and she immediately came to appreciate Natsume's warm personality.

Whoever named him, she thought Nobuhito—written with the characters for "believe" and "person"—was right on the dot.

Natsume loved children. Apparently, he'd gone into educational psychology wanting to become a schoolteacher and proceeded to grad school hoping to improve his ability to instruct and guide children.

Natsume hadn't become a teacher upon completing the program, however. He passed the A-level reform officer employment screening test and entered the Ministry of Justice. Kumiko thought she knew why Natsume had stopped trying to become a teacher and chosen instead to serve as a judiciary technical officer.

For a training visit during graduate school, they'd gone to a children's home in Saitama. It took in children who had no guardians, who faced abuse, or whose family had some hardship raising them.

There too, the kids immediately grew fond of the cheerful and gentle Natsume. Amongst them was a seventeen-year-old boy named Yoshio Hashimoto.

Yoshio had entered the home after suffering horrible abuse from his parents for a long time. He took a construction-related job when he was eighteen and left the home. Natsume was ecstatic about Yoshio as if he, himself, were becoming independent and making a new start. Apparently, he'd been taking the boy out for meals and lending an ear to his struggles. Half a year after leaving the home, however, Yoshio was arrested for manslaughter by the police. Not taking well to his boss's incessant bullying, Yoshio had struck the man. By some misfortune, he hit his head hard against a table as he fell and succumbed to internal bleeding.

If only he'd been closer to Yoshio and listened to his troubles more, it might not have happened, Natsume cried in frustration when he learned about Yoshio's arrest.

That case must have reoriented Natsume toward a career as a judiciary technical officer, who faced offending juveniles.

Kumiko was being inspired by Natsume before she knew. Up until then, she hadn't had much interest in children, but after finishing graduate school, she acquired qualifications as a clinical psychologist and decided to become a school counselor so she could be with kids and side with their hearts.

Hence her great shock that Natsume had entered the police force. That he'd become a detective, whose vocation was to doubt people, felt like a betrayal.

Why would Natsume have thought to become a cop? She was certain that a career doubting people was about the most unsuitable life for him.

The only reason that she could think of was that case.

About ten years ago, there had been a serial assailant in Nerima Ward whose victims were young girls. Natsume had appeared on TV as the father of one of the victims and made a tearful appeal to the criminal.

Please stop doing this, hurry and turn yourself in, he'd begged.

Natsume's daughter, who'd been attacked, fell into a coma—but Kumiko didn't know what had happened after that.

She'd known, from the time they'd all gone out drinking after completing graduate school, that Natsume had married and been blessed with a daughter. Looking at the TV screen, she'd recalled how proudly, and dotingly, he'd shown the photos of his family, and her heart had ached.

Did Natsume become a cop because of that? Did that case change him?

When Kumiko got home, she immediately looked through the morning paper.

Something had stuck in her mind when Natsume told her about the investigation.

The article was tucked deep in a corner of the local news section. The afternoon of the day before, a man had been found dead in a condominium in the third district of South Ikebukuro. The room showed signs of a struggle, and the corpse's head a traumatic injury. The victim was a twenty year old named Koji Sawamura.

It's all my fault! It doesn't matter what happens to me anymore!

When Kumiko recalled Yuka's words from the day before, goose bumps stood on her skin.

There was no way there was a connection. She shook the scenario from her head.

Hearing a knock, Kumiko raised her head. "Come in," she said.

The counseling room door opened and Natsume came in. "Sorry for bothering you at a busy time," he excused himself.

The anxiety that she'd suppressed the day before rapidly filled her when she saw his face. "I didn't think you'd invite me so soon to have that drink," she joked nevertheless.

"Sadly, until I solve the case we spoke about yesterday, that won't be possible," Natsume responded seriously to her forced attempt at humor. "I want to ask you about a student named Yuka Nakamura."

Her premonition had come true. She wanted to avert her gaze from Natsume but checked herself with great effort. At school,

Natsume had shown keen powers of perception. It wouldn't do for her body language to make him suspicious.

"When I asked her homeroom teacher Mr. Machida, he said you would know more..."

"What in the world do you want to ask?"

"What kind of girl she is...among other things. I need more information before I meet her."

"Why? Are you saying she's related to the case you talked about yesterday?"

"Unfortunately, I can't divulge any details about the investigation."

"It's confidential, you mean. Well, a counselor can't go around jabbering about things to do with clients, either. I'll get in trouble because it's a confidential relationship."

"You're quite right. Then let's talk a bit about the case. You'll see why I want to know more about her."

"Don't be standing around then, sit down so we can talk."

Kumiko offered him a seat on the room's sofa. She stood up and made herbal tea for the two of them. She wanted to calm down a bit before talking to Natsume. She placed a cup of tea in front of Natsume and sat across from him.

"Thank you," he said courteously and sipped the tea.

Kumiko also drank the tea slowly to quench her dry throat.

"First, let me briefly summarize the case. Yesterday afternoon, at around one thirty, the body of someone who'd died from unnatural causes was discovered in a condo room. The victim, a twenty-year-old man named Koji Sawamura, was found by a friend who came to visit him. There were signs of a violent struggle in the room. There were traces of the victim's blood on a table corner, so we believe that the cause of death was him hitting his head hard on the table. The estimated time of death is between nine in the morning to around noon day before yesterday."

Hearing that, she recalled Yoshio's case. It sounded like

manslaughter. That the victim hadn't been stabbed or strangled to death was a minimal relief.

"What kind of person was the victim?" asked Kumiko.

"I'm hesitant to say this about a person who's passed away, but frankly, he didn't have a good reputation."

"Didn't, how?"

"He has priors for assault. He appears not to have been gainfully employed lately, but was living in a nice condo. It seems that he was making money through various illegal means."

"Illegal means?"

"We're not sure what he'd been up to recently, but when he was last arrested, he had women he knew make date calls to men. He then blackmailed the ones who came. It's what's commonly called the badger game."

"So a lot of people have grudges against him."

"That might be so. The victim's wallet was left behind, so it doesn't seem to be a robbery, but his cellphone was gone."

"His cellphone?"

"Yes…the culprit must not want the victim's personal relationships to come to light, and so took his cellphone."

"So it might be one of the victim's acquaintances."

"I can't be certain, but the chances are pretty high. But even without the phone, we can look up the victim's call records and find out about his personal relationships. Within those records, we found Yuka Nakamura's number."

Natsume's words plunged Kumiko into a gloomy mood.

"Additionally, the rest of the students the school listed up for me yesterday had alibis."

Natsume uttering the word "alibi" felt almost surreal.

"With that, you probably understand why I want to ask about her."

"Yuka is a very insecure girl," Kumiko said, unsure how to explain things to him.

"Insecure?" Natsume leaned forward. His gaze indicated that he was quite interested.

"Over a year ago, she refused to come to school and started cutting herself. Day before yesterday, she even slit her wrists with a box cutter and was admitted to a hospital," Kumiko said, at which Natsume folded his arms in thought.

If a detective visited Yuka in that insecure state, what would happen to her? Kumiko couldn't help but feel extremely anxious.

Natsume lifted his face, looked at her, and said, "Would it be possible for you to come with me?"

Kumiko got into Natsume's car and headed to the hospital.

Having Natsume and Yuka meet now didn't sit well with her, but if Kumiko refused to accompany him, he'd no doubt meet the girl by himself. That was a detective's job. Kumiko thought it'd be better if she were there if the alternative was to leave Yuka alone with a detective.

"Could you wait a moment," she told Natsume in front of Yuka's room.

Natsume nodded that he understood.

Kumiko knocked on the door and opened it. Yuka was lying on her side on the bed facing the window. Her back was to Kumiko.

"Yuka, how are you?" Kumiko asked, but Yuka showed no sign of responding. Wondering if she was asleep, Kumiko got closer so she could see Yuka's face. She was awake. With a hollow expression, she was gazing out the window.

Seeing Yuka's state, Kumiko felt all the more apprehensive about the girl meeting a detective today.

Kumiko turned back to the door. Natsume was looking at them intently. When he nodded at her, she almost let out a sigh.

"Hey, Yuka… There's someone here who wants to talk to you for a bit," Kumiko said.

Yuka's eyes reacted, and she slowly turned her face towards the door.

"Good afternoon. Sorry for suddenly visiting you when you're not feeling well. I'm Natsume from the East Ikebukuro precinct. I'd like to speak with you a bit, if that's okay," Natsume said, stepping into the room.

Yuka started trembling visibly. "The East Ikebukuro precinct?"

"I won't take much of your time." Natsume took two folding chairs from along the wall, put them next to the bed, and sat down. He offered the chair next to him to Kumiko. "Yuka, you know a man named Koji Sawamura, don't you?" he asked.

Yuka just stared into thin air.

"Two days ago, Mr. Sawamura passed away. I wonder if you knew?"

She shook her head slightly.

"Is that right… I wonder what kind of friends you and Mr. Sawamura were. Most recently, you spoke with him five days ago on your cellphone," Natsume said, hinting that he already knew they were acquaintances.

"What kind of friends?" Yuka said in a small voice, as though squeezing out the words. "We weren't all that close. Sometimes he'd call asking, 'What are you doing right now?'"

"Have you ever gone over to his room?"

She shook her head.

"Do you know where it is?"

She nodded.

"I see… Day before yesterday, a little past ten in the morning, a girl wearing the same school uniform as yours was witnessed near the condo. It's a large, white building across from a park in South Ikebukuro. Does that ring any bells?"

"No…"

Natsume directed a piercing gaze at Yuka for some time.

Eventually, he stood up and said, "Thank you. If you remember anything, please contact me."

He left his card on the bedside table and exited the hospital room.

"Don't tell me you think she killed him?" Kumiko asked him after they left the hospital.

"It's our job to consider various possibilities. Even if it's something small, she seems to be hiding something."

Natsume halted and turned a piercing gaze at her. It was similar to the one he'd directed at Yuka. The man hadn't ever shown so razor-sharp an edge to Kumiko in the old days. Were these, then, a cop's eyes?

"Natsume…you've changed completely," she muttered wistfully. It was possible that the Natsume she knew was gone.

"You think?" asked the detective.

"Did you catch the culprit from that case ten years ago?" It was difficult asking about it, but she couldn't leave the question hanging.

"No, we haven't."

"And your daughter…"

"She's been in the hospital the whole time since then."

"Since then?"

Close to ten years had passed. What could have happened for her to be in the hospital even now?

"She's a vegetable."

Hearing this made Kumiko gasp and look back at Natsume. "Are you saying that you became a detective to catch the person who attacked your daughter?"

"That's about half of it," Natsume nodded, his expression unchanging.

"What about the other half?"

"I ran away."

"Ran away?" Kumiko repeated the words as a question.

"Do you remember Yoshio?"

"Of course."

"After Yoshio's case, I thought I wanted to become a judiciary technical officer who could help rehabilitate offending kids by properly facing their problems, the causes that had driven them to crime. But when my daughter became the victim of a crime, it shook my conviction to its core."

The sharpness in Natsume's eyes gave way to melancholy.

"Eyewitness accounts pointed to a minor as the perpetrator in that case. Day after day, I sat across boys who'd been sent to a juvenile detention center, and every time I did, I was seized by the feeling that the kid in front of me might be the one who hurt my daughter. As the days went on, my desire to help those boys ceded to a different emotion that was swelling in my heart."

"A hatred toward criminals?"

"Yes."

"You're saying that instead of providing support to kids like Yoshio, you chose to chase down criminals?"

Natsume dropped his gaze pensively for a bit, then nodded. He was biting his lip.

Perhaps a conflict was raging in him even now. It hurt to watch him like this.

"Sorry if I bored you."

With that, Natsume turned his back to her and resumed walking.

"So…what's behind her truancy and wrist-cutting?" Natsume asked as they got in the car.

"I don't know for certain. She won't talk to me about anything. But…"

Kumiko told him about Yuka's father being arrested by the police and her subsequent state during counseling.

"But after that she got better and could come to school again, right? Why did she stop and go as far as to cut herself?"

"I'm not sure if it's the cause, but a year ago, she was molested."

"Molested?"

Just as Kumiko had thought Yuka was at last regaining her cheer and attending school again, the girl had been groped on the train during her commute. She had complained, and a passenger had subdued the man and handed him over to a station attendant. Apparently the offender had been a middle school teacher who had a daughter around the same age as Yuka. When Kumiko had heard about that, she'd felt irate toward the man.

Following that incident, Yuka's spirits had sunk again. She said things like "I've become dirty" and started cutting her wrists with a knife. The encounter must have left an ugly scar on her heart.

"Despite scarring a girl's heart like that, the guy got a suspended sentence. Unbelievable, no?"

"So something like that had happened..."

When they reached the school gate, Kumiko got out of the car.

"Well, I'm going back to the station," Natsume said. "Thanks for today."

After watching the departing car for a moment, Kumiko went into the school.

Her cellphone rang as she walked to the train station, her day's work done. It was from Yuka's mother.

"Ms. Tanabe, it's terrible—" a shriek echoed in Kumiko's ears.

"What in the world happened?"

"There was a call from the hospital just now... They said Yuka...she disappeared from the hospital..."

Listening to the voice, Kumiko wanted to kick herself. How careless of her—

Having brought a detective to Yuka's room, she should have been on guard about what the girl might do.

"Okay," she said. "For now, please go home to see if Yuka is there. I'll go search around the hospital."

She hung up and ran toward the station.

She took the train to Hibarigaoka and headed toward the hospital by taxi from there. She'd said she'd search for Yuka but had no idea where to begin. For the time being, she walked around the vicinity hollering her name.

There was another call from Yuka's mother.

"Yuka…Yuka was…at home. She cut her wrists and there's so much blood coming out… What do I do…Yuka…Yuka!" the panicked mother screamed into the phone.

"Keep it together!" Kumiko shouted back at her, trying to calm her down. "Hurry and call an ambulance!"

"I just did…"

"Then I'll be waiting in front of the hospital. It'll be all right. Hold yourself together."

Hanging up, Kumiko headed to the hospital. After waiting outside for ten minutes or so, the sound of a siren approached, and an ambulance pulled up.

"Yuka!" She rushed to the stretcher that emerged.

"Yuka! Yuka!" the sobbing mother followed out, shouting her daughter's name.

The ambulance attendants rolled the stretcher into the hospital.

Yuka's face was pale as she slept on the bed.

A bright ray of sun broke through the window. Kumiko, not having slept a wink, gazed at Yuka's face.

Upon learning that she was in critical condition, her mother had collapsed on the spot, the strain of the last few days taking its toll. Currently she was asleep, hooked up to an IV drip, in a separate room.

Kumiko was helpless against the anger and frustration that welled up in her as she gazed at Yuka's sleeping face: anger at the girl's disregard of life and frustration at her own inability to save her.

Yuka slowly opened her eyes. When she looked around and saw Kumiko's face, her expression sank.

"Why…wouldn't you let me die," the girl muttered, partially raising herself.

Kumiko gritted her teeth at the words.

"I'm worthless alive… I'd be better off if you'd let me die."

Something snapped in Kumiko at that moment, and she promptly struck Yuka's cheek, hard.

"No one's life is worthless! Do you have any idea how many people you'll hurt by dying? Have you even thought once about how sad your mom will be?! If you really want to die then go ahead, but at least wait until your mom passes away," Kumiko let loose, glowering at the girl.

Yuka held her left hand at her cheek and stared at her counselor.

"Why are you suffering all alone?" Kumiko couldn't stop tearing up, try as she might. "Why won't you tell me anything? Am I not a support to you at all?"

"Ms. Tanabe…if you end up killing someone, how bad is the punishment?"

A chill ran down Kumiko's spine at the muttered question. Her vision was too blurry to make out Yuka's expression.

"My dad got sent to prison for as long as two and a half years on a bribery charge. If you've killed someone, how long do you have to stay in prison?"

Yuka's point eluded Kumiko. Was she confessing to having

killed someone? Kumiko was too afraid to ask and find out.

Sticking her right hand into her bedding, Yuka pulled out a business card that she seemed to have kept in her pocket and offered it to Kumiko. It was the one that Natsume had left there the day before. A phone number was written out on the reverse side.

"I want you to call the detective who was here yesterday," Yuka said.

"You mean Natsume?"

"If it's that detective, I feel like I can tell the truth."

"Why…him?" asked Kumiko.

"Because I think he'll scold me properly like you did just now."

Her eyes on the card, Kumiko hesitated. It frightened her to imagine what Yuka might say, but as her tears dried, she noticed that Yuka was looking at her earnestly. Kumiko took her cellphone out of her bag and called Natsume.

"He should be here in about an hour."

An oppressive silence filled the room as they waited; just as it was becoming unbearable, there was a knock on the door and Natsume came in.

For a moment, her eyes met with Natsume's. She thought they looked lonely.

"I'll tell you what really happened," Yuka said.

The detective quietly sat down in the folding chair that had been set up next to Kumiko and nodded at the girl.

"My dad was arrested about a year and a half ago. He worked hard for his family and was a really kind dad. I was too shocked by his arrest to care about anything anymore, and I stopped going to school and started going out every night. I even kept going to clubs and drinking until morning…and that's where I met Koji Sawamura. At first, he was a kind guy who just helped me forget my loneliness, but he made me do things I didn't want to do when I went to his room…"

Yuka paused and, instead of continuing, put her hand into her bedding and pulled out a phone. She pressed some buttons and handed it to Kumiko. It was the first time Kumiko had seen this phone.

The image on the display instantly made her avert her eyes. It showed Yuka in an obscene position.

"He took a lot of other photos and videos. If I didn't want them to be spread on the internet, I needed to do what he said. He forced me to do a lot of things I hated."

What kind of things had she been coerced into? Kumiko could more or less guess given that obscene picture, though.

I've become dirty.

Had Yuka been cutting herself out of the pain and self-loathing she'd suffered as a result?

"Ms. Tanabe always cheered me on, so I somehow kept trying, but as long as he existed…and had those pictures… Thinking that, I killed him. The fact that I have this phone is proof enough."

Kumiko's heart nearly froze at Yuka's confession.

She faced Natsume, who was sitting next to her and staring at Yuka. She sensed in his unblinking gaze neither the harsh edge of the day before nor the gentleness of the old days, but rather a will to gauge Yuka's truthfulness.

"But…I was wracked by guilt for having killed a person… I thought I'd atone for my crime by killing myself."

"That's not atoning for your crime, it's running away," Natsume said.

"I know. That's why—"

"Harming yourself doesn't atone for it, either," Natsume interrupted. "For that, you need to come clean about what really happened."

"What do you mean?" Kumiko asked him.

"The first time you cut yourself, weren't you trying to make amends to Mitsuo Iwasaki in your own way and coping with self-hatred for what you'd done?"

Yuka's shoulders twitched when she heard that name. Mitsuo Iwasaki—

Kumiko recalled hearing it somewhere before. Where? She frantically searched her memories and finally remembered. The man who'd been caught groping Yuka.

Amends to Iwasaki and self-hatred for what she'd done? What was Natsume talking about?

"What the heck? You've lost me," Yuka said, glaring at Natsume.

"You were ordered to frame Iwasaki for groping," the detective accused. Yuka's expression stiffened the moment he did. "Isn't that the thing you didn't want to do that Sawamura forced you into?"

"Wrong." Yuka frantically shook her head. "I never did anything like that…"

"Your first target was Mr. Iwasaki. Am I mistaken? As soon as you claimed you'd been groped, Sawamura would close in and get the target off the train, onto the platform, with the pretext of taking him to a station attendant. Then, he'd make a show of talking with you, still pretending to be a stranger, and threaten to turn the mark in to the police if he didn't pay up. If a woman claims that she was groped and she has a male witness, the victim really has no way out. But maybe because it was your first try, your timing was off, and an actual stranger on the train grabbed Mr. Iwasaki and handed him over to a station attendant. You ended up going to the police together and got stuck with filing a complaint against Mr. Iwasaki."

"That's not true!" Yuka denied vehemently.

"If it isn't, why are you covering for Mr. Iwasaki, a supposedly detestable man who groped you?"

Yuka looked at the detective dubiously. "Cover?"

"This morning, Mr. Iwasaki came to the police station to confess that he was the one who killed Sawamura," Natsume informed Yuka, who turned pale. "You must have been sick with guilt for what you'd done to Mr. Iwasaki. Yet, Sawamura kept on coercing you into fabricating gropings. There are no other records of you filing a complaint, so you must have succeeded at the blackmailing. Making up those cases, you came to cut your wrists from the guilt..."

Yuka hung her head at Natsume's words.

"I'll say it again... What you need to do to atone is to tell the truth."

Still hanging her head, Yuka didn't open her mouth.

"Yuka! Please do," Kumiko begged. She wanted to know what Yuka was really suffering from, to be able to support her, so she'd never contemplate suicide again.

"That day...encouraged by Ms. Tanabe and my mom, I thought I'd try and go to school. But I ran into Mr. Iwasaki on the way. He noticed me and followed me with a really intense look on his face. I rushed to get away, but he caught hold of my wrist in the park. Then, he frantically started pleading with me that he wasn't the one who'd groped me. I was seriously scared, but the moment he saw the scars on my wrists, his expression changed and he immediately let go of my hand. He was really kind and said I should stop doing it because my parents would be sad. He said he had a daughter around the same age and if he saw her looking like I did, he'd almost feel like his heart was being cut apart... When I heard him say that, I started crying right there."

Her eyes grew moist even as she spoke.

"He bought us juice at the park and we talked for a while. Thanks to my groping charge, he was unemployed and lived alone in a cheap apartment away from his wife and daughter. He said he was on his way to an employment agency to find work... but didn't say a single grudging word against me. Instead, he sympathized with me and said it was terrible that I'd been groped. But he swore that it wasn't him. If nothing else, he wanted me to know that. When I thought about his daughter, I couldn't stand it anymore. My dad getting arrested had been so painful for me… So I told Mr. Iwasaki the truth. I told him how I'd been blackmailed into making the whole thing up. I cried and apologized to him and told him I wanted to go to the police right then and testify that he was innocent, but if I did, that guy would…"

"And you told Mr. Iwasaki about the obscene pictures and your ongoing false accusations of groping?" Natsume asked, to which Yuka nodded.

"Then Mr. Iwasaki asked me where Sawamura lived… He said he'd talk to Sawamura and get back those photos. If he did that, he asked me, would I come to the police with him and tell them honestly that he hadn't groped me? When I nodded, he told me to wait there and headed to Sawamura's condo…"

"And you began to worry about Mr. Iwasaki and went to see how he was doing."

"When I arrived, I saw him coming out of Sawamura's room. I thought Mr. Iwasaki looked different from before, like he was afraid. When he started wiping the doorknob with something that looked like a towel, I had a bad feeling. After he left the condo, I went into Sawamura's room and…"

Then Yuka must have found Sawamura's body. She'd taken his cell with the loathsome footage and made herself scarce.

"If I hadn't done that…if I hadn't given Mr. Iwasaki his address, none of it would have happened. I trapped him not just once but twice. It's all my fault! I wish I'd never been born!" Yuka wailed.

"Mr. Iwasaki testified that when he met you, he was reminded of his daughter. He said he had to get those pictures somehow in order to prove his innocence, but even more, to eliminate the source of your continued suffering. But Sawamura was adamant about holding on to them. Not only that, he turned violent, grabbing Mr. Iwasaki by the collar. During the altercation and scuffle that ensued, Sawamura fell and ended up dying…"

Yuka lifted her head and looked at them. Her eyes were bloodshot.

"Mr. Iwasaki hadn't been able to confess to the police up until now, but he said he couldn't run from his mistake—if he kept running, he'd continue to make you suffer, so he turned himself in. You can't run from your own errors, either. I know it won't be easy for you, but will you talk about what really happened, to the police and at Mr. Iwasaki's trial?"

Stealing a glance at Natsume's profile, Kumiko was struck by his eyes. They were the same ones from their grad school days when he used to talk to kids with such passion.

"It's your responsibility, as well as your atonement."

Sniveling, Yuka nodded broadly.

"Well…the rest is your job." Standing up and clapping Kumiko on the back, Natsume left the room.

Kumiko immediately rose and chased after him. "Natsume—" she called.

The detective turned around.

"I guess you haven't changed much, after all."

Natsume laughed. "What, so I haven't grown?"

"I might say that," Kumiko returned with a smile.

She was still absolutely certain that no occupation suited Natsume less than being a detective. At the same time, just maybe, a cop like him wasn't such a bad thing.

A Cop's Eyes

"You know what, I'm not doing this..."

As the *izakaya* pub came into view, Seiji Tsukamoto lost his nerve and stopped walking.

"What are you saying, after coming this far? Everyone is looking forward to seeing you, Sei," his wife Kyoko pepped him up, pulling on his sleeve.

"But I feel bad toward your parents. We're having them take care of our kid while we go drinking. I'll go get Nozomi and take her home and then you can have fun for yourself." It was all an excuse to skip the coming party.

"They don't mind something little like this. They even said to take our time even if we don't get her tonight. Stop being a broken record. Let's go. You have to do some PR. Nozomi is going to need a lot of money and stuff from now on."

Kyoko steadily drew Seiji's hand towards the pub. Looking at the approaching sign, he let out a heavy sigh.

His middle school reunion was taking place in the pub. It seemed Kyoko regularly saw her classmates, but Seiji hadn't met with anyone in the eleven years since graduation. No, not even graduation. He hadn't been in attendance at the commencement ceremony, having gotten in trouble with the police.

As he thought over his many doings during middle school and seeing his classmates now, he felt heavy-hearted, like he was about to sit on a bed of nails.

"Welcome—"

He followed behind Kyoko as they were guided by one of the pub's employees.

Upon seeing the many shoes lined up at the entrance of the Japanese-style guest room, his feeling of tension reached a crescendo.

"Sorry for being late," Kyoko said. Hiding behind her, Seiji entered the guest room.

At that moment, the boisterous guest room suddenly quieted down. About twenty of his classmates were staring intently at Seiji. Although they were grown up and seemed more mature, he could remember everyone's names by their faces. Memories of his time in middle school flashed before his eyes, and he couldn't speak right away.

"Thank you…it's been a while…" he squeezed out the words, but everyone was still looking at him vacantly and hadn't reacted.

"Did everyone hear? Tsukamoto said 'thank you.' When did you learn those words?"

The moment a classmate named Sudo said this, everyone there was wrapped in laughter.

"Well…only recently," he replied, and the laughter doubled as he scratched his head.

A classmate in the middle of the room opened up a seat for them, and Seiji and Kyoko sat down side by side.

He ordered a beer and had a toast with everyone. One by one, everyone came to his side, curious, and poured for him. Still not knowing what to talk about, Seiji drank his beer and chimed in occasionally.

After some time, his nervousness seemed to have subsided and he was able to talk with everyone normally.

It seemed he had been needlessly anxious. To everyone right now, it seemed the trouble Seiji had caused in school was nothing more than old memories.

"More importantly, who ever thought the class chair Toda, of all people, would marry Tsukamoto?" cajoled Hashimoto, who had been studious and reserved in their middle school years. He seemed to have judged that Seiji had been safely defanged after talking to him for a bit.

"Yeah? Even back then, I felt like they had feelings for each other. But Tsukamoto was always busy fighting and just didn't have the time for dates," Tomomi Sekiguchi, who was still close to Kyoko, poked some more fun at them.

Seiji meekly lowered his head. "I'm really sorry for how I was back then... I caused everyone a lot of trouble."

"You sure were rough. We were scared, so all we could do was avoid you...but everyone sympathized with you in their hearts," said Nishikido, who'd had the best relationship with Seiji out of everyone there.

Unable to say anything in return, Seiji put his glass to his mouth.

"Looks like the party's getting on—"

Seiji turned toward the entrance and the shrill voice that seemed to extinguish all their boisterousness.

A man threw off his shoes and stepped up into the guest room. Looking at him, Seiji realized that it was Ohta.

The moment Ohta entered, Seiji felt the atmosphere change. Everyone watched Ohta with distant eyes and started whispering to their neighbors.

Seeing that, he guessed that Ohta was an uninvited guest.

Showing no sign of noticing everyone's stares, Ohta looked around the room and smirked. He sat down in an unoccupied seat and poured himself a beer, which he started drinking.

"Who invited him..." Nishikido muttered with an annoyed look on his face.

"I think no one did," Sekiguchi answered coolly.

"Did something happen with Ohta?" asked Seiji, not understanding the shift in mood.

"Well, until recently, we invited him to our reunions…but the way he acts and talks is so strange, it's creepy…and we've been leaving him out."

"When you say he acts and talks strange…"

"Look at that face for yourself," Nishikido told Seiji, which he proceeded to do.

Ohta was grumbling and muttering to himself, all the while sneering and looking around. The moment their eyes met, Seiji felt like he'd witnessed something disgusting and averted his gaze.

"It feels like something's off with him, doesn't it…"

Just as Nishikido said, the look in his eyes wasn't normal. Tugging back his memories from middle school, Seiji remembered Ohta as a gloomy and somehow irritating guy. He had been teased often, by Seiji and the rest of the class.

During elementary school, he'd sometimes gone to Ohta's house to play, but at some point, as far as Seiji was concerned, he'd become a nuisance.

"You know that case from a long time ago…where a man who'd been picked on went to a reunion and killed all his classmates? When I see that guy I get the chills."

"He wouldn't…right?"

When Seiji looked next to him, Kyoko's expression was taut, too.

"What's that guy been up to?"

"Apparently, ever since he dropped out of high school the freshman year, he's been a hermit. If you've been living that way for a decade, I guess that's what you become…"

Come to think of it, he had heard about this from Kyoko in the past.

She had been in the same cram school as Ohta during middle school, but after summer break of their freshman year, he'd stopped coming. She'd said there was a rumor at the cram school that he'd also quit high school around that time.

"Well, let's not mind him and have fun. By the way, what have you been up to, Tsukamoto?"

"Oh...I started bartending when I was twenty, and I finally opened up my own place this past year."

"Oh, that's amazing. Can I come by sometime?"

Seiji, who had anticipated this, pulled a business card holder out of his pocket.

"'Hope'...that's a good bar name," Nishikido said looking at the card.

Seiji thought it was a bit of a cliché but had decided on it because it described his current self best.

"It's just a small, counter-only shot bar in Ikebukuro, but if you can, please come. I'll give you a discount."

When Nishikido stood up to announce that Seiji had opened a bar, everyone came to him asking for a card. Handing them out, he felt a foreboding presence at his back. When he turned around, Ohta was staring at Seiji with a faint sneer.

"All right, who's coming to the after-party?" asked Sudo, standing up and taking attendance.

"It's our bad, but we need to go get our daughter, so we'll bow out. Today was fun. We'll come again," Seiji told everyone and headed out of the room with Kyoko.

"Tsukamoto," a voice came from behind as they were putting on their shoes. Goose bumps ran down Seiji's back. When he turned around, it was, of course, Ohta standing there.

With a viscous gaze, he put out a hand. "Give me a card, too."

Seiji was reluctant, but he couldn't resist the guy's ghastly gaze, which seemed to coil around him.

"See you then..." Card in hand, Ohta smiled faintly and waved at them.

"Sei—" Kyoko called for his attention, and Seiji rolled his eyes to the side. "A penny for your thoughts."

"Well, it's nothing...I'm just tired," he answered, but since they had gotten into the taxi, he'd been thinking over his middle school years.

"You didn't need to worry, right?"

"Yeah...it feels like some lump in my chest I had for eleven years just went poof." He was grateful towards Kyoko for forcing him to attend the reunion.

"Good," she said, faced the other way, and closed her eyes.

Her face had been so tense before the party, and now she looked exhausted. There was no mistaking that it had been a stressful day for her as well. It was still some time until they got to her parents' home in Nakano. He would let her sleep until then.

Absentmindedly watching the scenery run by outside the car window, he retread the thoughts that had been racing through his head.

Everyone sympathized with you in their hearts—

He hadn't noticed at all back then, but perhaps everyone who'd been aware of his home environment had felt that way.

It certainly called for sympathy.

From the time Seiji was a child, his father was in and out of jail for theft, assault and battery, and meth use. Even now, his father was in the middle of serving a ninth sentence. During the times his father was in prison, his mother would bring home a new man, and when he was fourteen, she disappeared somewhere.

Seiji was a troubled kid since he was very little. He hurt people around him as though they were to blame for his unhappy home. In elementary school, he was taken to a child consultation center for shoplifting and for taking other kids' pocket money. By middle school, he was an inveterate delinquent who stole and got into fights day after day, a hot potato tossed among the police, juvie, and family courts.

During that time, he thought his fate was completely sealed. In the same way that he could not change his parents, he could never swap out the violent blood coursing through him.

He was convinced that being born to his parents was the root cause of everything.

But he now thought that there were no excuses for many of the things he'd done, whoever his parents were.

The person who convinced him of that was none other than Kyoko.

He'd been in the same school as her since elementary. Raised in an upstanding family, Kyoko did well in school ever since she was a kid and enjoyed the trust of her teachers and classmates. He didn't remember now how he'd come to know her, just that even when he caused problems and was feared by everyone, Kyoko never ceased to be considerate toward him.

He'd had something of a crush on her ever since they were kids, and felt at times that she liked him back.

At the age of sixteen, however, without saying anything to her, he skipped their hometown. He simply couldn't abide living there anymore. From then on, he moved from job to job, occasionally getting his hands dirty with things he shouldn't have, and somehow made a living.

He reunited with Kyoko when he was twenty. By chance, she'd come to the bar he was working at then. She was with her friends, and he at the counter, but when their eyes met, her lips trembled, as though robbed of words, and the next moment she started crying. Then, leaving her friends behind, she ran out of the bar.

Seiji had thought over what those tears meant. Had she been overcome with the joy of being reunited with him? He writhed between the part of him that wanted to believe it and the part that didn't want her to show up again.

Several days later, Kyoko reappeared at the bar.

She asked him why he'd vanished without telling her anything. Seiji, however, could only answer that he'd come to hate their town.

He couldn't possibly tell her the true cause of his antipathy—about the grave sin that he had committed.

After that, she paid him many more visits.

The twenty-year-old Kyoko was pretty enough to be mistaken for someone else. The slight crush Seiji had always had on her grew and grew, but it felt wrong for him to announce his feelings. Unexpectedly, however, Kyoko confessed to him that she had always liked him.

Even as Seiji felt a soaring sense of happiness, his heart ached with pain.

Going out with Kyoko meant living in sight of the cross he'd been burdened with.

Could he bear that suffering? If she weren't at his side, he might be able to live with his eyes averted from his sin. Just as he'd done until then. But another part of him pleaded to him from deep inside.

That this was the fate he deserved.

That enduring the pain of having his heart gouged out as long as he lived was his atonement. Even on the brink of death, he wouldn't be able to turn a blind eye to the sin he'd committed. He might build a happy home with Kyoko and, all the while, continue to suffer in his heart. That had to be his punishment for eluding the police.

With such a resolve, Seiji started dating Kyoko.

Although he did, because of his guilt he couldn't bring himself to touch her. Kyoko, despite having confessed to him, also seemed to be hesitant about something and maintained a distance.

Perhaps, having confessed as an extension of her childhood crush, she wasn't sure if a man like Seiji were right for her after all.

Once they started dating, he sought to live an honest life like a man reborn. He plunged himself into the bartending work that he had only thought of as a temporary gig and worked hard to become a man Kyoko would approve of.

In the end, it took close to two years for their hearts and bodies to yield and meet.

Although their relationship held and blossomed, Kyoko's parents strongly opposed marriage. Their familiarity with Seiji's home environment and missteps as a teen proved to be a real obstacle. They married nevertheless three years ago, a fact that Kyoko's parents refused to accept for some time, but Nozomi's birth two years ago finally swayed them.

The warm family Seiji had yearned for since childhood surrounded him now. He relished his happiness, but it would forever be entwined with heartache.

"It was your reunion, you should have stayed longer," reproached Kyoko's mother, Nozomi in her arms.

When Seiji looked at Kyoko, she made a face as though to say, *See?*

Kyoko's mother looked regretful as she handed Nozomi over to her daughter.

"Um…before going to the reunion, we bought some sweet dumplings from the department store so could I set them out as an offering. I heard from Kyoko that Yasuko liked them."

"Oh, we're always troubling you."

Kyoko's mother consented, however, and Seiji went into the living room.

He placed the dumplings on a plate Kyoko had brought him and set them as an offering on the family shrine. He sat in the formal position and faced the death portrait. A sweet-looking girl with a smile looked back at him.

Kyoko's little sister, Yasuko, had passed away when she was eight, the victim in a certain decade-old case.

Whenever Seiji saw the portrait, the pain threatened to sunder his heart in two.

He closed his eyes and put his hands together.

I'm sorry—

He continued to pray for forgiveness from a girl he'd never met.

"Welcome—"

When Seiji turned his eyes to the door and saw the patron, his face almost turned into a grimace.

Ohta was eyeing the bar's interior and approaching the counter.

The eight seats at the counter were mostly filled with regulars. Taking the one empty seat, Ohta sat down, faced Seiji, and smiled faintly.

"Hey…welcome. You came so soon… Thanks," Seiji said, controlling his discomposure as he put a coaster in front of Ohta. "What would you like?"

"To think you, Tsukamoto, would be polite to me. Back then, you'd just call me 'dolt' or 'bastard' or 'dimwit.'"

The regulars glanced at Ohta.

"Well, I'm in the hospitality business. I was…also immature back then," Seiji dodged smoothly.

"I'm fine with anything, just give me something strong," Ohta ordered in the most ill-tempered manner.

"How about bourbon on the rocks?"

Why in the world would he come here—

Seiji had a bad feeling but poured some ice and bourbon into a glass and set it in front of Ohta.

"A name like 'Hope' doesn't suit you, but this is a pretty good bar… Maybe I should have you let me work here."

That would be no joke—a cheerless man like Ohta at the counter would doom the business.

"Speaking of which, Ohta, you haven't been working? You were always smart, there must be plenty of jobs for you," Seiji countered for the time being with flattery so naked that it got on his own nerves.

"No social rehabilitation for me. All thanks to you..."

The regular next to Ohta looked at him and Seiji.

"Hey, listen up," Ohta started speaking to the regular in an overfamiliar way. "This guy screwed up my life. In elementary and middle school, he always bullied me in the nastiest way. Because this guy kept stomping on my self-confidence, I'm still scared of talking to people."

True, Seiji had often beat up Ohta whenever he was in a bad mood. His past self would have done so on the spot now, but with his customers watching, he couldn't do anything at all.

Ohta, apparently not sated, informed his fellow guests of the many wrongdoings that Seiji had perpetrated in his middle school days. The regulars who were forced to listen embarrassedly asked for their checks one by one.

"Enough!" Seiji snapped at him after the last customer had left.

Ohta was grinning, clearly pleased by his host's exasperation. "What, it's the truth, isn't it?"

"If you're going to bring up all that, you're obstructing my business, so don't come back."

"I'm afraid I can't oblige. I like this bar, so I'll come and have fun every day."

"Don't."

"You have no right to say no." The malice in Ohta's eyes made Seiji recoil a bit. "You said that a lot when we were in school. When you told me to bring money or to strip in the classroom, I'd cry and refuse...and you'd always say that."

"Look, I'm sorry..." Seiji indeed might have been that horrible towards Ohta back then.

"Hey, you're letting me down apologizing so easily. The fun is only just starting."

"The fun?"

Ohta took a scrap of paper out of his pocket and tossed it onto the counter. It seemed to be a copy of a newspaper clipping.

Another Girl Attacked—

Seeing that large, uppercase print was almost enough to stop his heart.

"You remember, don't you? Those cases that happened in our neighborhood," Ohta said, smiling. "Two innocent girls were attacked one after another with a hammer, and one died."

"I remember. That was really unpleasant..." answered Seiji, careful not to betray his unease. Feeling agitated, however, he stepped away from Ohta and started hitting at ice with an icepick.

"I was watching."

At those words, Seiji's hand jerked and the pick hit his own finger. Barely registering the pain, he looked at Ohta.

"When you smacked the girl's head with a hammer."

Seiji's vision shook as though he were blacking out as he met Ohta's eyes. Leaning on a shelf behind him and narrowly avoiding sinking to the floor, he managed to retort, "I did nothing of the sort."

"I believe it was the first case. You were wearing a black sweatshirt with your hood on. Initially, you were wandering around the park, but then you hit a girl's head with a hammer and ran away. A thug like you, attacking such a sweet girl."

He had been seen—to think that Ohta had witnessed him back then.

"I've got proof, too."

"Proof..."

"This is becoming fun. Maybe I'll have another drink," Ohta touted his glass.

"Why didn't you report it to the police?" Seiji put ice in the glass with shaking hands, then filled it with bourbon.

"That would have been boring."

"Boring?"

"Yeah...back then, you were the notorious delinquent. A familiar face at the police and juvie, right? But you were still a minor. Getting arrested back then wouldn't have been that big of a blow given our country's laws, but I wonder about now. These past ten years, I was sincerely hoping you'd win happiness. Otherwise, it wouldn't be fun when you're caught."

Seiji saw Kyoko and Nozomi in his mind's eye.

"Still, to think you'd get married to Kyoko, of all people... When I heard about it, I was actually stunned. I wonder how she's gonna take it when she finds out," Ohta rattled on gleefully.

Kyoko's sister, Yasuko, had been killed in an apparent case of random violence that followed. Based on the M.O. and eyewitness accounts, the papers had reported that the same culprit must have struck again. But Seiji hadn't assaulted Yasuko.

"It wasn't me for Kyoko's sister," Seiji squeezed the words out.

Ohta smiled, unperturbed. "And who would believe that?"

"What the hell do you want?" Was it money? He didn't have any to spare, but...

"Let's see... I bet you don't have much in the way of cash. How about you loan me Kyoko for a night."

Seiji's reaction was to glare at Ohta.

"Stop with the scary face... I've had a thing for her since we were in elementary school. I've wanted to sleep with her, just once. If I could slobber over that woman, I'd forgive and forget everything. I promise I'll even hand the proof to you."

"Don't screw with me."

"Just one night will do. If I told the police, your family would fall apart, wouldn't it? Kyoko wouldn't want that, either, I bet. So ask her for me? My feeling superior for being with your woman is all it's gonna take to end your problems."

Ohta smiled and stood up.

"I'll come again, so open a tab for me."

With those closing words, he left the bar.

Clenching his teeth, Seiji looked down at his hand. It was gripping the icepick hard.

He raised his head in surprise at the sound of the door opening. A regular had come into his bar.

"Sorry, but…I don't feel well and was closing for tonight."

After putting an ice scoop into his bag, Seiji left the bar and headed towards the main street.

"Up to Hikarigaoka park please," he told the taxi driver when he got in.

What should he do—

He felt like he was going mad from his mounting sense of panic.

There was no way he could offer up Kyoko to that man for a night. First of all, what did Ohta think Seiji could even say to ask her?

But if he didn't let Ohta sleep with Kyoko, he might give the police evidence of the crime he'd committed.

If it came to that, Seiji would be arrested as the assailant. It wasn't just that. He might be accused of killing Kyoko's sister, though he hadn't committed that crime.

Would the police believe that he wasn't Yasuko's killer? If they ended up not believing him and pinning her murder on him, just how much of a shock would that be to Kyoko and her parents?

When the taxi stopped, he impatiently received his change and ran into the park ahead. He relied on his memories as he fervently searched around the dark park.

After looking for some time, he finally found a place that matched them. He'd dug a hole under the thickly growing trees before his eyes and buried the hammer there. Heading to a particularly large tree within the thicket, Seiji pulled out the ice scoop and started digging. No matter how much he dug, however, the hammer failed to materialize. There was no mistaking he'd buried it there. He didn't remember digging a hole deeper than now, either. Afraid of keeping the hammer on him, he'd come to the park, a short distance from where he'd attacked the girl, to bury his weapon.

Perhaps Ohta, who had witnessed his crime, had gone as far as to follow him here.

Then, he'd dug up the hammer Seiji had buried.

But Seiji didn't think the hammer would be decisive proof. The girl's bloodstains might have been on it, but before burying it here, he'd wiped the handle many times. His fingerprints shouldn't be on it.

Unless there was evidence other than the hammer—

How...he thought, then something came to mind.

Ohta had been into photography back then and was always carrying a camera. He might have documented the critical moment on film.

Amidst the pitch-black darkness, Seiji looked up to the heavens.

"Welcome home. You must be tired."

Kyoko, who had opened the door, turned to him with a smiling face.

"Yup..."

Seiji's bar was open until four in the morning. After that, he cleaned up and came home around six in the morning. In order not to incur Kyoko's suspicion, he'd killed some time at a family restaurant next to the park and come home at the usual hour.

When he came in, the tabletop was set with breakfast. Because they couldn't have dinner together, they at least tried to make sure that they had breakfast as a couple.

"Sorry...but I don't have an appetite today."

"Are you not feeling well? Now that you say so, you look sort of pale..." Kyoko asked him, worried.

"It's nothing, really. But...I'm dead tired, I need to crash."

Looking at Kyoko's face was so difficult that he immediately went into the bedroom. Nozomi was still asleep in her small bedspread. Crouching next to her, he stared at her peaceful, sleeping face.

Ohta wanted to rob him of what was irreplaceable and dear to him. Out of revenge for being bullied, the man intended to make not only Seiji but his entire family miserable.

Whether he acceded to Ohta's demands or rejected them, the joy of having this warm household would likely crumble away.

What should he do—

His mind raced as he looked at his daughter's sleeping face, but no answer came to him.

Yet...no matter what, he couldn't let go of this happiness.

Seeing a police vehicle a little ahead of them, Wataru Nagamine told the driver, "Around here will do."

When the taxi parked, he scanned the surroundings of the house that was the crime scene. There was already a large crowd of onlookers.

Nagamine paid the driver, got out of the car, and headed to the scene. He showed the uniformed officers his badge and passed through the cordoning tape. When he looked at the front entrance, a man he recognized was standing outside.

Nobuhito Natsume—

"Thanks for joining us," Natsume noticed Nagamine and called out to him.

"Can we go inside yet?"

"They're in the middle of forensics. It seems it'll take a while."

"Then let's do some questioning until then."

Natsume nodded and followed after him.

For about an hour, they went around asking neighbors about the victim. When they returned to the house, forensics had finished and they could go inside.

When they entered, there was a stairway right by the entrance. They could hear several voices coming from the upper level. It seemed the scene of the crime was on the second floor. Climbing up the stairs with Natsume, he made for a door that had been left open.

Nagamine hesitated a bit before stepping in. It was a very large room, but apart from the bed against the wall, there was almost no space to put a foot down thanks to all the objects scattered about. Plastic model boxes, DVDs, obscene comics, and magazines seemed to almost bury the man who had collapsed facedown.

Subsection Chief Yabusawa and one of the forensics staff were standing huddled together in a clear spot.

"Hard at work," Nagamine called out.

Yabusawa turned to face them. "This was your jurisdiction, wasn't it."

He'd said this to Natsume, who was behind Nagamine. Yabusawa didn't look pleased in the least. Natsume was notorious even at Investigation Section One for being an oddball.

"Can we come in?" Nagamine asked.

"Yeah. Forensics is done, and you can't do your job out there, can you."

Nagamine did his best to walk on tiptoes and not step on anything inside as he went in.

Natsume followed, also doing the same.

"Wow, what a crazy room. The cause of death was..." Nagamine crouched down and peered at the man's face.

"Strangulation," answered Yabusawa. "It seems like the victim's neck was constricted with a phone cord or something. He must have put up a lot of resistance for the room to end up like this.

"It seems that the victim, Toru Ohta, had been a shut-in for the last decade. The first person to discover him was his mother. She noticed the living-room window was broken when she came home from work. She said she was worried and knocked on his door, but didn't get a response and came in to find him in this condition."

Indeed, interviewing the neighbors earlier, they'd turned up very few memories of Toru Ohta.

The Ohta family had moved to Zoshigaya about five years ago, apparently from Nerima Ward.

"There's something that bothered me a little," the forensics staffer said, lifting up a bag from the bed.

"Bothered?" Nagamine repeated, looking at the bag.

"There was a hammer in this plastic bag. It seems to have a lot of dirt on it, but the head looks like it has bloodstains on it."

"There was also a towel and a container with a USB in the bag," noted Yabusawa. "Could you go to the station from here and check what's on the USB?"

"Understood."

Nagamine took the bag and turned to leave the room, but Natsume stood unmoving, his gaze fixed on one spot.

"What is it?"

"Excuse me."

Natsume got on the bed and lay on his belly. He reached his hand toward a gap in the shelves behind the bed. However, the opening was so small, his hand wouldn't fit.

"Is there something like a stick?" Natsume raised his head and asked.

Nagamine looked around and found a thirty-centimeter ruler on top of a shelf. "How about this?"

Natsume jabbed the ruler between the shelves and tried to fish something out. An object that glittered in the light emerged from the gap. Natsume grabbed it with his white glove and showed it to everyone. It seemed to be a hair ornament made of beads. A heart and the name "Yasuko" were embroidered on it with multicolored spheres.

Arriving at the East Ikebukuro police station, Nagamine and Natsume headed to the assembly hall on the third floor where the investigation headquarters would be.

When they entered, the precinct detectives were in the process of moving chairs and long desks to set up the HQ.

"Computer?" Nagamine asked, to which Natsume replied, "There." They made for a desk placed along a wall.

They started up the laptop and put in the USB. On it were eight photos, which they brought up on screen. What were these?

It seemed like a park. The focus was on someone's back. The person was wearing a dark sweatshirt with the hood up and seemed to be in the middle of running in the opposite direction. In the corner, a surprised woman faced them. The moment Nagamine glanced at the bottom of the picture, Natsume butted in ferociously, brushing him aside, and moved the cursor. The picture expanded. They could see a small child collapsed on the ground.

"Emi…"

Nagamine turned toward Natsume, who had uttered the name, his face pale as he stared at the screen.

"Are you okay?"

Nagamine examined his partner, who sat next to him. Although Natsume gave a firm nod, Nagamine got a lump in his throat guessing at what the man was going through.

The photo in the possession of murder victim Toru Ohta indeed showed the moment Natsume's daughter, Emi, had been attacked ten years ago. The other seven likewise captured the moments before and after the attack. While none of the photos showed the face of the hooded person, the hammer held in his right hand indicated that he was, without a doubt, the culprit. They corresponded with eyewitness reports of the serial assailant cases from back then.

Of the eight pictures, just one showed a woman in one corner. Although Nagamine wasn't certain, she had to be one of the witnesses he'd spoken to.

He remembered the hair ornament found in Ohta's room.

That was likely the second victim Yasuko Toda's. In each of the cases, a girl had been struck in the head with a hammer and robbed of her hair ornament. The culprit must have taken something as a way to commemorate the deed, as criminals who did it for the pleasure were sometimes known to. The crimes' M.O., eyewitness accounts that a young man had been seen running away at the precise hour, and the victims' missing hair ornaments pointed to a common perpetrator for the two cases.

They made no mention of the missing hair ornaments to the press. They'd kept it confidential as a detail only the culprit would know.

Why had the ornament been where it was discovered? Had it been hidden in the bag with the hammer and somehow fallen out?

Regardless, they had retrieved from Ohta's room a hair ornament thought to have been on Yasuko Toda and a hammer with evident bloodstains.

Nagamine chewed over the fact, anxious for the investigation meeting to begin.

When a hush overtook the assembly hall, Nagamine looked

toward the door. Yabusawa and the other chiefs came in and sat in the front row. The initial investigation meeting was on.

First, they announced the results of the forensic autopsy of the victim, Toru Ohta.

The cause of Ohta's death was suffocation; he had been strangled with a cord-like object. The estimated time of death was between fourteen and sixteen hundred hours that same day.

Then came a report from an investigator who had conducted interviews. As of now, there were no witness reports from the Ohta residence's vicinity that might lead to an arrest.

"Next—"

At Subsection Chief Yabusawa's voice, Nagamine stood up.

"A bloodstained hammer, towels, and a container were found in a bag in Toru Ohta's room. Inspecting the photos on the USB found in the container, we found that they depict a serial assault case from ten years ago—" Nagamine reported.

The hall suddenly burst into a commotion. Most of the investigators were looking at Natsume, who was sitting next to Nagamine.

"In addition, we believe that the hair ornament found in Toru Ohta's room belonged to Yasuko Toda, one of the victims from ten years ago. Toru Ohta may be related in some way to the incidents back then, and for that reason we ask for a DNA test on the bloodstains on the hammer as well as Toru Ohta."

Although there was no physical evidence from the first attack, the culprit had thrown away a glove with Yasuko's bloodstains near the crime scene after the second attack.

If the DNA from the bodily fluids inside the glove showed a match, Ohta would be the perp of the unsolved decade-old serial assailant case.

But—Nagamine thought as he sat down in his seat.

If that was the case, what were those photos?

The camera had captured the culprit. Ohta had them. Did

that mean that Ohta wasn't the one who'd attacked Emi Natsume? Or had someone else taken those pictures and given them to Ohta? A blackmail scenario—

When the investigation meeting ended, Natsume was called over by the chiefs, who were discussing something in the front. They probably wanted Natsume to excuse himself from this investigation.

It had a bearing on the spree that his daughter had fallen victim to. He wouldn't be able to make composed decisions.

Nagamine, himself, valued Natsume even though the man was just a precinct detective, but it would be best if other investigators handled the case at hand just this once.

Nagamine was thinking this as he watched, but Natsume shook his head and seemed to be making an earnest appeal. Then he came back.

"Want to grab something to eat?" Nagamine invited him.

"I think they have a point." Pouring beer into Natsume's drained glass, Nagamine tried to persuade him.

After finishing their meals, Nagamine had expressed his agreement with the brass about Natsume removing himself from the case this time, but the man would only stubbornly shake his head.

Nagamine had felt so during the last investigation too, but Natsume was pretty stubborn despite his gentle demeanor.

"It might become a very painful investigation for you."

"For me, investigations are always painful," Natsume quietly answered.

That had to be true. If his own family were killed or hurt in a case, Nagamine wasn't sure he could stay at this job. He'd be unable to put a lid on his hatred for any and all criminals.

Yet, Natsume had done the opposite and jettisoned his prior career to become a cop.

Nagamine admired the man's resolve. He also understood why Natsume balked at removing himself from the investigation, but without exception, having a personal interest in a case was taboo.

"This time is different, it'll be even worse. First of all, if Toru Ohta did attack your daughter…would you be able to pursue his killer with the right amount of anger and determination?"

"Yes," Natsume nodded. "The culprit who attacked Emi must be caught, and the same goes for the murderer who killed the attacker."

"What if, like you, the suspect is related to one of the victims of the serial assailant case? Would you be able to go after the perp without letting your emotions interfere in any way whatsoever?"

"Of course," Natsume replied firmly.

"Ow—"

Preparing ice for his clients, Seiji had struck himself in his hand again with his pick.

It was normally easy work he could perform like a machine, but tonight, his hand kept shaking and it wasn't going well.

"Bartender, that's unusual for you," a regular sitting at the counter peered at him and said.

"Even monkeys fall from trees or whatever it was," he responded jokingly, but his mind was a vortex of anxiety.

The night before last, Ohta had come to the bar again.

He'd grinned and taken a seat away from the other customers.

"Did you talk to Kyoko?"

While Seiji hung his head, Ohta had pulled an envelope from his bag and put it on the counter.

"The evidence is in here, so hurry up and ask her."

"I can't do that… I honestly regret having bullied you. Let me make it up to you some other way."

Ohta had sneered at the words Seiji had squeezed out.

"Don't worry, I'm sure Kyoko will do exactly what you tell her to. I mean, it'd be to protect her precious family. If you tell Kyoko that, I'll tell you something interesting."

"Something interesting?"

Ohta had left the bar laughing, not deigning to reply.

Seiji had wanted to check what was in the envelope right away but couldn't leave his customers unattended. He'd finally examined the contents after closing time.

The photos in the envelope had chilled him to the bone. They documented the very moments he'd committed the crime—

When he got home, however, he still couldn't bring himself to convey Ohta's demand to Kyoko. Tossing and turning in bed, he kept thinking about what he should do, but no matter how much time he agonized over it, there was only one answer.

That was it. If he wanted to protect his happiness, there was no other way.

Having arrived at a conclusion, he sat up in his sheets.

When he came out of the bedroom, Kyoko got a curious look on her face and asked him, "What's wrong?" Usually he slept until noon and only left at around one. When he checked the clock, it was still a little after nine.

He lied that he had to go buy new equipment for the bar and went out. He called a taxi and headed to Hikarigaoka.

He remembered that both of Ohta's parents worked. If they still did, the only one home would be Ohta. If he waited for the chance, he might be able to pull it off. He frantically rehearsed his plan in the cab.

When he got to Ohta's house in Hikarigaoka, however, there was a different name on the nameplate. It seemed they had moved.

He sent Nishikido a message asking if he knew where Ohta lived now and got back a response in the afternoon. It gave an address in Zoshigaya in Toshima Ward.

What do you need it for?

To Nishikido's question, he answered, *Ohta came to my bar yesterday but forgot something, I'm delivering it to him*, and immediately headed to Zoshigaya.

When he arrived at the address in the message, he did indeed find a house with an "Ohta" nameplate. When he looked at his watch, it was past three.

Was Ohta or his parents home?

To find out, he rang the doorbell, but there was no response. After ringing the bell several times and confirming that no one was home, he readied himself.

He put on some gloves and went around to the back of the house. He grabbed a large rock from the garden, shattered the glass of one window, and broke in. It was the living room. He went around to the other rooms on the first floor, but none of them was Ohta's. He went up the stairs to the second floor and opened the three doors there one by one.

When he opened the last door—

He didn't want to recall the scene that had greeted him.

Too flustered by it to achieve his goal, he had fled down the stairs and out the living room window in a panic.

"Bartender, check."

He was brought back to reality by a customer's voice.

"You seem kind of absentminded. Are you still not feeling well?"

"Sorry."

Lowering his head, Seiji returned the change.

As the customer left the bar, Seiji put both hands on the sink and let out a heavy sigh.

Had he been witnessed by someone? No, it wasn't just that. The police would target Ohta's acquaintances. Nishikido might tell the police that Seiji had asked for Ohta's address yesterday.

And if the police found the photos and data from the serial assailant case…

He heard the door opening and raised his head. A first-time patron wearing a suit had come in.

"Welcome…"

When a second guest followed in, Seiji held back a gasp.

Espying him at the counter, the man also stopped in his tracks with a surprised look on his face.

Natsume—

"Sorry for coming at such a busy time. We're Nagamine and Natsume, metropolitan police. We would like to ask you some questions."

The first man showed Seiji his badge.

Metropolitan police?

Confused, he looked between the badge and Natsume, who was standing in the back.

Seiji doubted his eyes, wondering if he was hallucinating. More than the police visiting him so soon, he couldn't believe Natsume was standing before his eyes.

But apparently it was no illusion.

"Tsukamoto," Natsume recalled Seiji's name.

"You know him?" the man called Nagamine asked.

Natsume nodded slightly as they approached the counter.

"Actually, we came to ask you about this man." Nagamine put a picture on top of the counter.

The moment Seiji saw Ohta's headshot, he was brought from his trance-like state back to reality.

"Toru Ohta. Do you know him?"

"Yes…of course. We went to the same elementary and middle schools. I was surprised when I saw the news this morning."

Since learning of Ohta's murder in the morning, Seiji had been terrified as though he were being hounded by a terrible demon, but he tried not to betray his fear as he replied.

"So he was your classmate… Mr. Ohta had a business card for your bar in his wallet, and that's why we came to visit. When did you last see him?" Nagamine asked.

If he told a bad lie, it would only come to haunt him later. "The last time was the night before last. We met for the first time in a while at a reunion and I told him I'd opened a bar, so he came to visit a few days later…"

"At that time, what did you talk about?"

"Well…Mr. Natsume here should know this well, but I was wild in my teens…and he had a lot of complaints about me bullying him back then. I told him it'd be on the house and he went home happy in the end… He even dropped in the next day."

"Did he say that anyone had a grudge against him? Or do you remember anyone like that?"

"If there was, he didn't tell me…and I hadn't seen him for eleven years until that reunion. I have no idea what kind of people he was associating with now."

"During elementary school and middle school, who was he closest to?"

"I wonder…I don't remember much. To be honest, even though we were schoolmates, I didn't have much in common with him."

"Lastly, where were you between one in the afternoon and the evening?"

This was probably what they called an alibi. "I was at the bar. Normally I arrive at two, but I wanted to try making a new cocktail."

"That seems difficult."

"Probably not as much as being a detective. Even though we weren't close, we were classmates once, so please do catch the murderer."

"Yes. We will conduct our investigation with every means at our disposal. Thank you for your cooperation," Nagamine said, then headed to the door. Natsume bobbed his head and followed suit.

"Um—" Seiji called out without thinking. The duo stopped and looked at him.

"I'll wait outside," Nagamine said to Natsume and exited by himself.

Checking Seiji out, Natsume's expression loosened. "It looks like you're working hard."

Although Seiji had called him back, he didn't know what to say. "So, the metropolitan police department…" he just narrowly managed to utter.

"About ten years ago, I changed jobs. You've gotten pretty polite," Natsume ribbed him.

Why—Seiji thought to ask and stopped. He knew the reason better than anyone. It was in order to catch Seiji. There was no mistaking why Natsume had quit being a judiciary technical officer; he'd joined the police force to catch the culprit who'd attacked his daughter.

Beyond that, there was one other thing Seiji wanted to ask.

What had become of Natsume's daughter? It had been reported in the news that the victim, Emi Natsume, had sustained a serious wound to her head, but Seiji didn't know even now how she'd fared since.

If she'd recovered from her injury and was healthy, he might feel that much less guilty.

"Back then…you appeared on television, right? You said that your daughter was the victim of some crime."

"Yeah."

"And now your daughter is…"

"She's been in the hospital ever since."

"When you say that… It's been like ten years."

"She's become a vegetable."

Vegetable—the word stung deep into his heart.

"I'll come by again when I have the time."

Natsume smiled and left the bar.

As soon as the man was out of sight, Seiji crouched where he stood as though all of his strength had been sapped away. Tormented by despair, he covered his face with both hands.

Vegetable—

Emi's adorable face as she turned when he was about to hit her with the hammer flickered before his eyes and would not leave him.

For ten years, while Seiji had been cobbling together a happy life, that girl had never recovered and lived as though she were dead.

Why had he ever—

If he could, he wanted to go back in time. He wanted to go back to those days and engrave, deep in his heart, the words that Natsume would speak to him. Then this wouldn't have happened.

The first time Seiji met Natsume was when he was fifteen.

Arrested for assault right before graduation, he'd been sent to a juvenile detention center near his home. There, the person in charge of interviewing him was Natsume.

The centers investigated the family environment and personal relationships of juvenile offenders and what had driven them to resort to crime. There were almost daily interviews with judiciary technical officers.

Seiji was always flippant during them.

He didn't mind getting stuck in a reformatory. Even if he left, there was nowhere for him to go.

No matter what happened, his nature would never change. It was all because he'd been born to those parents of his.

But Natsume refuted everything Seiji said.

He couldn't let his hatred towards his parents and society

consume him. No matter what hardships he came across, he could overcome them if he had the strength. Natsume wanted Seiji to cultivate the strength to face those hardships from now on.

Seiji was persistently met with such niceties. One by one, Natsume's words got on his nerves until he could barely stand it.

What did the guy know about Seiji? There were things in the world that stayed the same no matter how much you struggled. He, Seiji, might be young but already knew this. How dare someone raised without knowing hardship dole out that shit, like he knew better.

While he was at the center, his loathing toward Natsume grew and grew.

Even after he left, his hatred didn't subside at all. Convinced that he had nowhere to go, and nothing to do, whether or not he finished middle school, his despair may have been entwined with everything else back then.

No longer able to contain the rage blooming in his chest, he bought a hammer at a hardware store and, concealing it on his person, followed Natsume as he returned home from the detention center. He was ready to attack if Natsume wandered into a dark spot. But the chance never arrived, and Natsume entered a housing complex near the center.

Seiji watched with frustration from outside the complex as the man climbed the stairs and was welcomed home by a woman who poked her face out of the door. The bastard smiled happily as he embraced a child who'd also come out.

The moment Seiji was treated to a glimpse of the warm household, an impulse surged from deep inside him.

The reason the guy could spout such idealistic nonsense was that he was happy. He couldn't begin to understand Seiji's feelings.

The following day too, Seiji went out to the complex where

Natsume lived.

When a woman and a kid emerged from the unit he'd singled out the previous day, he slinked after them. Natsume's child was a girl. On her long, black hair was a pretty hair ornament. When they got to a nearby park, the woman and girl started playing.

It was a happy scene of a child with her parent. The warm family that he'd never had—

Gazing at the scene, he was helpless against the rage that overtook him.

Then, a thought dreadful and repulsive even to himself raced around in his head.

For having spouted all that stuff to him, Natsume needed to learn the meaning of hardship. When he did, he'd see things Seiji's way, without a doubt. He'd understand true despair, which made it impossible to face such hardship. He'd know hate, which nested deep in your heart and lived there as long as you did.

When the girl strayed from her mother's side and headed to the shade of a tree, he followed after the kid. Checking his surroundings to make sure that no one was near, he approached her from behind and called out to her. The moment she turned towards him with a smile, he hit her head with the hammer.

When the girl started to collapse face-first to the ground, he unconsciously reached out his hand and supported her head. Then he laid her down. An endless stream of blood was issuing from where he'd struck her.

He'd done something horrible. He felt anything but calm, but noticed that his fingers had touched the girl's hair ornament.

He might have left fingerprints on it—

Snatching it from Emi's head, he slid the hammer under his belt and ran for his life. When he recovered his wits, he was gripping the ornament, stained with blood, in his left hand.

The incident was covered widely. As Seiji watched the news in fear, Natsume came on TV as the victim's father.

Stop this—please don't rob kids of their future—face what you've done, and hurry and turn yourself in—

The man's tearful pleading brought no satisfaction whatsoever to Seiji. A hollowness clung to him and wouldn't let go.

He didn't need to be told by Natsume. He didn't intend to do such a thing again. Yet, a week later, another assault that copycatted Seiji's occurred.

Kyoko's younger sister, Yasuko, had died as a result.

"Last night, I got contacted by Tomomi."

Seiji's chopsticks paused and he lifted his face to Kyoko's words.

"I was asked if we were going to Ohta's funeral..."

Last morning, Kyoko had frozen from the shock of seeing Ohta's case on the news, but now she seemed much calmer.

"That's right...even though we weren't close, he was our classmate," Seiji answered, averting his eyes from Kyoko. He stretched his chopsticks towards the cooked fish in front of him.

He didn't have much of an appetite, but if he acted strange with his wife, she might sense that something was off.

If Kyoko learned that Seiji was involved and that he'd been visited by detectives at the bar, what would she think?

He brought his eating utensils to the sink and went to the bedroom. He changed into pajamas and slipped under the covers laid out next to Nozomi.

These past few days, he hadn't been able to sleep much. If he didn't rest at least a bit, neither his body nor his mind would bear up.

As he stared at the dim ceiling, the door opened and Kyoko came into the bedroom. Without saying anything, she joined him under the covers.

"What...are you sleepy?" he asked, finding it odd. Usually, while Seiji slept, she would clean or wash or play with Nozomi.

"Sei, make love to me."

Kyoko hugged him under the covers.

"We'll wake Nozomi."

"It's fine. I want you to fuck me."

Kyoko kissed him. She slid her hand into his pajamas and caressed him aggressively.

"Sei, I love you…"

She sucked on his lips like she was starving.

Seiji was a bit bewildered by her behavior.

For half a year, they hadn't enjoyed that kind of intimacy. There was no specific reason, but Seiji had been awfully busy since opening the new bar, and Kyoko had been tired from Nozomi's childcare as well as other things, and they'd naturally stopped being together physically.

It was the first time, ever, that Kyoko had initiated it with such passion, though.

It'd been a while, and his body ached to hold her, but thanks to his anxiety over Ohta, he couldn't get in the mood.

"Sorry…I'm tired today…"

Seiji detached himself from Kyoko and pretended to sleep.

"I wonder what it's like being a shut-in for ten years…" Nagamine couldn't help muttering. He looked at Natsume, who was in the driver's seat.

"I wonder, too. It might be like being in prison… Maybe it's even lonelier."

At his partner's reply, Nagamine faced forward again and let out a small sigh.

They were three days into the investigation but hadn't made much progress.

No matter how much they looked into Toru Ohta's contacts, no acquaintances with a motive to kill surfaced. The guy didn't even have a cellphone. Why had Ohta, who lived mostly refusing to make contact with anything outside his room, been murdered?

They had even thought of it from the perspective of a robbery, but it was difficult to rule out some tie to the assailant case from ten years ago.

"It seems to be over there."

He looked to where Natsume pointed and saw a signboard on the first floor of a building. "Direct Staff Service": the business handled direct-mail advertisements to households.

According to their canvassing of nearby residents, no suspicious person had been witnessed visiting Ohta's house. The investigators were conducting an exhaustive search of door-to-door and newspaper delivery services, among other leads.

Natsume and Nagamine got out of the car and went to visit the company. They stated the purpose of their visit to a man who said he was the supervisor.

"That area's postings are handled by a woman called Ms. Fujimoto," the supervisor told them after sifting through some documents.

"Where is she now?" Nagamine asked.

"Who knows. We asked her to work today, but there isn't a specific mailing time..."

"Please tell us her contact info."

As they approached the convenience store, they saw a woman standing in the parking lot.

Pulling up there, Nagamine opened the car door and greeted the woman.

"Are you Ms. Fujimoto?" he asked.

The woman nodded, looking slightly bewildered.

"Sorry for bothering you while you're working. We're from the police. Would you talk to us inside the car?" he said, showing her his badge.

Fujimoto got into the back seat. They had gotten her

cellphone number from the supervisor at Direct Staff Service and arranged to meet at a convenience store near the Ohta residence. Nagamine immediately laid out a map of the neighborhood and summarized their business to her.

"I did make deliveries in the area that day…but I don't think I saw any suspicious people," she answered.

"Sorry, but could you actually come to the house now?"

They drove the car out of the lot and towards Ohta's house.

"It's here…"

They got out of the car and stood in front of the residence. Nagamine asked for her impression.

"I did come here. That reminds me, I saw a woman visiting around that time."

"A woman?"

"Yes…a man opened the door and invited her in. It almost seemed like he was dragging her in, grinning."

"Was it this man?"

They showed her a photo of Toru Ohta, and she nodded yes.

"Around what time was this?"

"It was…after one, I think. I don't remember the specific time…but it was between one and two."

Slightly before the estimated time of death. Nagamine, unable to hold back his excitement, leaned forward a little as he asked, "What kind of woman was she?"

"She was young and pretty. This might be rude, but the man seemed a little gross and…I remember very briefly wondering what kind of relationship they could possibly have."

At the evening investigation meeting, the forensics personnel stood up and started giving their report.

"First, we'd like to share that we found DNA on the victim's body and genitalia that was not his."

In that case, Toru Ohta might have had intercourse with a

woman before being murdered.

Nagamine remembered what Fujimoto had said earlier. Shortly before the estimated hour of the crime, Ohta had let a young and pretty woman into his home. What sort, though? Perhaps it was rude, just as Fujimoto had said, but Nagamine couldn't imagine Ohta having that kind of relationship with a woman. She might have been a sex worker.

"Continuing on, Toru Ohta's DNA matched that from the glove used in the assailant case ten years ago. We also confirmed the bloodstains on the hammer to be from Emi Natsume and Yasuko Toda."

This set off a clamor in the hall.

Nagamine glanced at Natsume, who was sitting next to him. Natsume wore a taut expression and had his gaze fixed straight ahead to conceal any distress he might be feeling.

The course of action that the investigation section chief announced for the next day onwards took the forensics report into account.

First, they'd continue to pursue the robbery line and leads on Toru Ohta's contacts. In addition, they were to look into the assailant case victims' families acting on their grudge; the chance that Ohta had an accomplice; and the possibility that he might have been blackmailed with those photos.

It was the worst development imaginable, Nagamine thought.

From here on out, Natsume would be putting his efforts into apprehending the murderer of the perp who'd assaulted his daughter. Moreover, it required targeting a family who had been hurt, like his own, and whose child had died.

Would Natsume really be able to keep his cool like he'd said?

When the investigation meeting ended, Nagamine was called over by Yabusawa.

"Starting tomorrow, you'll look into Yasuko Toda's relatives," Yabusawa said, his tone bitter.

"Yes."

"You, though, can't get on his wavelength," cautioned Yabusawa, no doubt referring to Natsume.

"Understood."

"Don't you feel reluctant?" Nagamine asked.

Natsume, who was in the driver's seat, glanced at him. "About what?"

"We're going to see people who're in a position similar to yours. What's more, you need to suspect them."

Natsume and his wife Minayo's alibis had been confirmed the day before; he'd been at the East Ikebukuro precinct investigation section, and his wife had been visiting their daughter's hospital. Other investigators were confirming Minayo's family's alibis as they spoke. Natsume was an only child, and apparently his parents had passed away in a traffic accident when he was young.

"I asked for it," Natsume let drop.

"You did?"

"I requested the station chief to put me on investigating the other victim's family if Toru Ohta turned out to be the culprit of the assailant case."

"Oh? So then…"

"When I asked him to consider the work I've done up until now, he said he understood."

Wow—Nagamine understood why Yabusawa had had such a bitter look assigning the task to them.

"I have one thing to add to our conversation from the other day."

"What…"

"I was wrong when I promised you that my emotions wouldn't interfere even if the victims' relatives ended up being suspects."

"Wrong?"

"If it was the victim's family...I can't say that I don't sympathize. I do, as someone who suffered the same sorrow. But I'd never forgive the crime it made them commit."

Nagamine couldn't take his eyes off of Natsume's profile for some time.

Yasuko Toda's parents lived in a house in Nakano. Ten years ago, they had been living in Nerima; perhaps the trauma of the case had made them move away.

Facing the Todas' doorbell, Nagamine hesitated a little.

Having investigated the case back then, he'd interviewed Yasuko's family about many things. He remembered how the parents and the high school sister had wept. To think that he'd meet them again under such circumstances...

"This is the police," he said, pressing the bell.

The door opened to a woman peeking her head out. It was Yasuko's mother. He remembered her as having jet-black hair, but now, a decade later, her hair was completely white.

"What does the police..." she began, perturbed. Then she seemed to recognize Nagamine. "You're the detective from back then..."

"It's been a very long time."

"It's the detective from the case...honey!" she hollered, her face changing color, and the father came out from the back. He had also grayed and wrinkled to an unthinkable extent over the long days and months.

"Actually, we think we may have identified the assailant from the case ten years ago," Nagamine told them.

The couple looked at each other in surprise.

"What kind of person was it?!" the father demanded, looking ready to pounce on him.

"It was someone living in the neighborhood back then named Toru Ohta. Do you know him?"

It seemed the husband didn't. His wife, however, mumbled the name and eventually looked back at Nagamine.

"Toru Ohta… It can't be… The boy who was in the same middle school as Kyoko?"

"That's right."

When Nagamine nodded, the mother looked like she might collapse on the spot, all of her strength gone. Her husband quickly caught her.

"Why would he…why would that boy do that?! He was in the same cram school as Kyoko and even came over and played with Yasuko…"

The mother started crying madly.

"Toru Ohta was murdered this Wednesday. We are investigating the case," Natsume said, stepping forward, as though to take on the most unpleasant part.

"Murdered?" the father asked, his eyes opening wide.

"Yes. I am very sorry, but we would like to know where you were Wednesday, from afternoon to evening."

"You think we killed him?" There was anger in the father's voice.

"No, that's not it. We just need to check," Natsume replied, holding fast.

The two reluctantly gave their alibis. The father said he'd been at his workplace in Marunouchi except during lunch break. The mother had apparently been at home the whole time, but around three, a neighbor had come to visit and they'd had tea together for some time, so it was nearly impossible for her to be the culprit.

"Does your daughter live here?"

"Our daughter got married."

"Could you please tell us where she lives?"

When the mother gave their daughter's address and the husband's name, Natsume's expression changed a shade.

At the sound of the doorbell, Kyoko walked over to the interphone.

As Seiji watched, her expression grew grimmer.

"Who is it?" he asked after she was done talking.

"The police… I wonder why."

She looked anxious as she headed to the front entrance.

No—could they be coming to arrest him?

Although his body was frozen with terror, he couldn't let Kyoko face them alone. Seiji took a deep breath and headed to the entrance.

Natsume and Nagamine, who'd also come to his bar, stood outside the door. Back then Nagamine had taken the lead, but this time it was Natsume who stood in the front facing Kyoko.

"Sorry for bothering you at a busy time. You may know already, but we're investigating Mr. Ohta's case. We would like to ask you some questions."

Seeing Natsume's expression, Seiji relaxed a little. They didn't appear to be here to arrest him, at least not right now.

"Yes… Such a thing happening to my former classmate… I'd like to help in any way I can," Kyoko answered.

Natsume proceeded to ask much the same questions that had been put to Seiji at the bar. When was the last time she'd seen Ohta? Could she think of anyone with a grudge against him?

The last time she'd seen Ohta was at the reunion, she replied, and she didn't know anyone who had a grudge against him, not having known him all that well.

"Well, this is something we ask everyone, but where were you on Wednesday between one o'clock in the afternoon and four o'clock?"

"That day I must have…had my mom look after my daughter, and gone out to do grocery shopping." Kyoko gave a department store's name, apparently remembering where.

"I see."

Natsume's expression unexpectedly softened. Wondering why, Seiji turned around to find Nozomi walking towards them.

"Nozomi..." Seiji picked up his daughter.

"So your name is Nozomi. I wonder how old you are?"

"Two."

Natsume reached out his hand and tenderly caressed Nozomi's head. He seemed to be examining her hair ornament.

"That's a cute hair ornament. Did your mom make it?"

Kyoko answered, "Yes. It's just cheap beads, though."

"You're quite skilled. I'd love for you to make one for my daughter. Did you also happen to make this one?"

Natsume pulled a hair ornament out of his pocket and handed it to Kyoko.

As she stared at the hair ornament, she seemed to be holding back tears.

"Yes...I made that for Yasuko..." she squeezed out the words, and closed her eyes. When she opened them again, her tears spilled out.

"Why do you have that?" Seiji asked.

"There's something we need to report to you. We believe we may have identified the culprit who attacked Yasuko. It was Mr. Toru Ohta, who has been murdered."

At those words, Seiji looked at Natsume in shock. "You're kidding..."

He couldn't think of anything else to say.

"The DNA gathered from the things the culprit left at the crime scene where he attacked Yasuko matched Mr. Ohta's. It seems there's no mistake he was the one who killed Yasuko."

When Seiji looked over at Kyoko, she was gazing at Natsume with a dumbfounded expression as well.

"As a result, we need to trouble your parents, unfortunately. They might be shocked if we contacted them out of the blue.

Would you be kind enough to give them a heads-up?"

"I understand," Kyoko nodded.

"With that, excuse us."

Natsume made a small wave at Nozomi. His eyes looked somewhat lonely, Seiji thought.

The moment the door shut, his anger at Ohta made his body shake. Perhaps sensing his rage, Nozomi, whom he held at his chest, started crying.

"Give her to me."

Kyoko held Nozomi in his stead.

Why had Ohta copycatted him and attacked Yasuko?

He knew right away. It was revenge against Seiji. Ohta must have attacked the family of the one person Seiji had been close to, just to fan his guilt. So he could never come near Kyoko again. He couldn't think of any other reason.

To think you'd get married to Kyoko, of all people—

Remembering Ohta's smirk, he felt like the blood in his entire body was freezing over.

It was terrible... Yasuko hadn't been murdered by chance, it was all Seji's fault.

"That detective...I feel like I've seen him somewhere before," Kyoko muttered.

"He was the father of the first victim."

Kyoko looked at him, her eyes wide with surprise. "Sei, do you know that man?"

"Yes...he looked after me a bit once upon a time."

"Looked after...at the police?"

"No, back then, he was my judiciary technical officer at juvie."

"And his daughter is now..."

"Apparently, she's been in a hospital ever since. She became a vegetable."

Looking at his daughter as his wife held her, he desperately held back his brimming tears.

At the sound of the bar door opening, Seiji lifted his face.

Natsume lightly raised his hand and came in. "Good evening. Are you still open?"

"Yes…"

If he could, he didn't want to see Natsume, but he had no reason to turn him down.

Natsume sat in the middle of the empty counter. Trying not to peer too much into the man's eyes, Seiji placed a coaster in front of his guest.

"What would you like?"

"Right…how about a bourbon soda. I can't get too drunk."

Seiji took a glass from the shelf behind him and filled it with ice. He poured in bourbon and soda, mixed them, and placed it in front of Natsume.

The detective raised the glass and sipped.

Unable to bear the silence, Seiji joked, "If you can loaf around at a place like this, the investigation must be going well."

"Not so. My workplace is close, so it's just a nightcap."

Seiji was left with nothing in his hands, so he turned his back to Natsume and started polishing the bottles on the shelf.

"And I also wanted to come here privately once. It's a nice bar."

"Thank you very much," Seiji accepted with no intonation.

"You had the strength to pave your future."

At those words, he couldn't but turn around.

Natsume was gazing at him with a wan smile. The man seemed genuinely glad, and Seiji's chest ached relentlessly.

"Did you become a detective because of what happened to your daughter?"

"Yeah…"

"Then your goal's been fulfilled since you found the culprit who attacked her. Too bad you couldn't hurt him with your own hands…" Natsume stared at him intently at this. "Wouldn't it be best if you went back to your old job?"

He thought that being a detective didn't suit Natsume. Or rather, he didn't *want* Natsume to be doing this type of work. Digging up people's lies, incurring hatred while pursuing suspects, all that didn't suit him. In the same way Natsume had done for him, he wanted the man to continue to be someone who approached people laid low with despair and pointed out the correct path.

Natsume had been a good juvie officer, the first adult worthy of respect that Seiji had come across. He believed that now, from the bottom of his heart.

"I can't, really… I'm also paving a new path. Struggling all the while," Natsume said. Then he fell silent, as though engrossed deep in thought.

During the long silence, Seiji remembered the favor Kyoko had asked of him. He pulled a small paper bag from the shelf drawer and put it in front of Natsume.

"Kyoko said to…give this to you if I saw you."

Natsume opened the paper bag and pulled out the hair ornament inside. He gazed at the accessory Kyoko had made.

He had to be thinking about his daughter—

Natsume looked over at Seiji.

"Lastly…the same bourbon, but straight."

His laugh was forlorn.

They were heading to the Tsukamotos' condo, with Natsume driving.

Nagamine glanced over at his partner, but Natsume's eyes were fixed forward and his lips were pursed. The man had been silent since the morning investigation meeting had ended.

"Are you sure about this?" Nagamine asked.

Natsume responded with a barely perceptible nod but didn't speak.

"We don't have to be the ones. There are plenty of other investigators. At least you—"

"I'm fine."

Saying just that, Natsume maintained his silence for the rest of the way.

When they got out of the car, they waited for the men in the second vehicle to come out before stepping into the building. The investigators, four including himself, headed to the third floor, where the Tsukamotos lived. When they arrived at the door, Natsume immediately reached his hand out to the doorbell.

They heard the voice of the wife and mother, Kyoko: "Coming!"

"This is the police. May we enter?" Natsume announced.

After some time, the door opened, and Kyoko poked her head out. Soon, Tsukamoto, who was holding Nozomi, also emerged from the back.

There were four investigators at their door; the couple clearly seemed to sense that this wasn't normal.

"Is there…something you need?" Tsukamoto asked with a stiff expression.

"Mrs. Kyoko Tsukamoto…we would like you to accompany us to the police station for questioning," Natsume stated.

The couple looked at each other.

"Hey, what is this about? Why does Kyoko have to go to the police?!" ranted Tsukamoto, beside himself. Nozomi, whom he was holding to his chest, started crying furiously.

"Sei, calm down," Kyoko soothed her husband's nerves. "Detective, may I just get a coat?"

"Yes," Natsume replied with a nod.

Tsukamoto, dumbfounded, watched his wife's back as she disappeared into a room inside. She immediately came back wearing her jacket. Before putting on her shoes, she gently caressed Nozomi's head. The girl hadn't stopped crying.

"Sei, take care of Nozomi," Kyoko told her husband, her eyes showing resolve, and stepped out of their home. Flanked by two investigators, she headed to the elevator.

"Well, then..." Even Natsume seemed to have no words beyond that.

When his partner made to close the door, Tsukamoto rushed toward him and held his sleeve.

"Wait a second! Why does Kyoko have to be taken by the police? If she's going, I'm going too!"

"You need to be with Nozomi, don't you?" Natsume reminded him.

"Do you even have a warrant? Why do you need Kyoko..." Tsukamoto pleaded, close to tears.

"No arrest warrant has been issued yet. She's just a person of interest at this moment. On the day of the incident, she visited Toru Ohta's house and had a physical relationship with him."

When Natsume said this, Tsukamoto's expression seemed to turn to stone. "What...the hell are you talking about... Why would Kyoko...get into a relationship with that guy..."

"The bodily fluids on Ohta's genitalia matched her DNA. We used a strand of hair from the ornament she gave me. It must have gotten there when she put it on her head to see how it looked."

Tsukamoto's eyes widened in disbelief. "You...used the gift you got from Kyoko..."

"That's right," Natsume answered, brushing off Tsukamoto's hand and heading to the elevator.

Seeing Yabusawa enter the assembly hall, Nagamine stood up from his seat and hurried over.

"How was it?"

The subsection chief shook his head with a sour look. "She's decided to remain silent, no matter what we ask. She says she'd talk to Natsume."

Taking in Yabusawa's annoyed response, Nagamine turned around. Natsume sat at a desk, his head propped up with both hands, as though he were pondering something.

"What shall we do?" Nagamine asked Yabusawa, facing towards him again.

"What else? But he's a fellow victim. Keep an eye on them so it won't be an easy deposition."

Nagamine nodded. Walking over to Natsume, he called out, "Let's go," at which his partner pursed his lips and stood up.

Exiting the hall, they headed to Interrogation Room 1. When they opened the door, Kyoko, who was sitting behind a desk, lifted her face in surprise.

"From now on, I will do the questioning," Natsume said, sitting across from her. Nagamine took his seat at another desk by the door, his eyes on his partner's back.

"To start… On the day of the murder, you visited the home of Toru Ohta, is that right?"

Kyoko, her gaze fixed on Natsume, nodded.

"Around what time?"

"Sometime after one."

"What did you go to his house for?" Natsume asked.

Kyoko twisted her lips as though she found it funny. "You know the answer…an affair."

"Since how far back have you had such relations with him?"

"Half a year or so? We ran into each other in the street and since then… You know how my husband works at night. I occasionally found an excuse to leave Nozomi with my parents and met with my lover."

"I can't bring myself to believe that you started a relationship with Ohta of your own volition… Were you forced into it?"

"No. It was what I wanted. For the past six months, I haven't had that kind of relationship with my husband. I begged, but he'd always say he was tired or whatever... Ohta might not have looked it, but he was actually quite amazing in bed," Kyoko offered up with an obscene smile.

"Aren't you hiding something? Didn't he force you into a relationship by using some secret against you?"

"It was nothing like that. I'm telling you the truth. I came here completely ready, and I won't lie. I understood when I called my parents after your visit. You'd marked me."

Marked? What is she talking about? wondered Nagamine.

"In that short time," Kyoko continued, "you figured out that I was Ohta's killer, didn't you?"

"I wasn't confident. I am, like you, the family of a victim. Remembering people who're dear to you, it's possible to lose yourself. But seeing that hair ornament, wouldn't you normally ask where I'd found it or who'd kept it? So I thought maybe you already knew who Yasuko's killer was..."

"And you laid a trap for me. You wanted to find out whether or not my parents had shared with me that Ohta was the culprit... In any case, I was prepared, since all you needed to do was marshal evidence. Still, not knowing exactly when you'd come was unbearable..."

"Could it be that...you left the hair on purpose?" Natsume asked, to which Kyoko nodded.

"Yes...because I thought you would then feel responsible to the end. If I had to be interrogated anyway, I wanted it to be by someone who felt my pain."

"You're admitting that you killed Ohta?"

"Yes."

"Why did you do such a thing..."

Kyoko, who'd spoken in a flat tone until then, replied with a near shout. "How else can you make someone who commits a crime and doesn't feel a smidgen of remorse pay for it except with his life?!"

Then she continued, "Right after having sex with that man, I found a hair ornament in a gap between some shelves. The man who killed Yasuko had just been holding me and enjoying himself. He'd slept with the family of someone he'd murdered without feeling a shred of guilt. At that moment, I was filled with a murderous urge that I couldn't hold back. While he lay there satisfied after playing with me, I wrung his throat with a telephone cord. I remember that man's eyes widening in surprise, and he resisted with everything he had, but Yasuko lent me her strength."

Hearing this, Natsume shook his head. "Yasuko wouldn't wish for that."

"That's not true! I bet you agree in your heart. You may never be able to say it as a detective, but you must be thrilled down deep that he's been murdered. The man who took a hammer to your daughter's head and left her a vegetable is dead," the words flooded out of her as tears streamed down her cheeks.

Then, Kyoko just laid her head down on the desk and started sobbing. With her in such a state, it would be some time until the interrogation could resume.

"Natsume, maybe we should take a break," Nagamine suggested.

Natsume nodded, stood up, and joined Nagamine by the door. When they opened it, Yabusawa was in the hallway.

Peeking in for a read on the situation, the subsection chief asked, "How did it go?"

"She confessed to the murder," assured Nagamine.

"Is that right? Then let's move on the arrest warrant."

"Could you wait a little longer?" requested Natsume, eliciting a dubious look from Yabusawa. "I think she hasn't told us the truth."

Nagamine was inclined to agree that Kyoko was hiding something.

He just couldn't believe that Kyoko would have an affair with Ohta. As Natsume said, she might have been forced into it on account of some secret. If so, what dirt had Ohta had on her?

He thought for some time but came up empty.

"Chief—" An investigator came running toward them from the other end of the hallway.

"What is it?"

"Seiji Tsukamoto just turned himself in. He says he was the one who killed Toru Ohta—"

"What?"

Nagamine and Natsume couldn't but meet each other's eyes.

Even now, his mind was in chaos.

Staring at the door in front of him, he begged his heart to hurry and calm down for what was to come.

After Natsume and the others left, Seiji desperately tried to make sense of what was transpiring around him, but it was impossible. He couldn't wrap his head around his wife being taken by the police, and he certainly had trouble swallowing what he'd been told about Kyoko and Ohta.

The two having an affair was unthinkable.

Yet, they'd detected Kyoko's DNA on Ohta's body and genitals according to Natsume.

It was not something he could accept. Kyoko had been canoodling with Ohta right before Seiji's break-in?

He'd trespassed into the guy's room to steal the evidence from the assailant case.

What he'd seen upon opening the third door, however, was Ohta's body, collapsed and buried among magazines and plastic model boxes.

Holding his breath, Seiji had crouched down and checked on

Ohta. The guy was dead—

Had Kyoko really killed him? If so, what should Seiji do now?

If she had done it, the motive would have been revenge for Yasuko, but he had been the cause of everything.

If he hadn't attacked Natsume's daughter, Yasuko wouldn't have met such a fate.

Nevertheless, Kyoko was being accused of a crime while he was getting off free. He absolutely couldn't let that happen.

Having made up his mind, he entered the bedroom. He raked through the closet and deposited in his pocket something he'd never thrown away. Leaving home with Nozomi, he took her to Kyoko's parents, then went to the police intending to put the whole case to rest.

The door opened, and Natsume and Nagamine came in. Nagamine went to the desk by the door, while Natsume sat directly across from Seiji.

"They said you turned yourself in..." Natsume began after staring at Seiji for some time.

Facing the man across a desk like this reminded Seiji of juvie. He'd been interviewed by Natsume in just the same manner, but he wasn't the irresponsible kid he'd been then. Now, he had dear ones that he'd protect no matter what.

"That's right... The police has made some sort of mistake. The one who killed Ohta was me," he said defiantly.

"She already confessed to murdering Ohta."

"It's to cover for me, isn't it?"

"Rather than you coming here to cover for her?"

"That day, using a rock, I broke into Ohta's house through the living room window. Isn't that what the police call 'an investigative secret'? They withheld that bit on TV and in the papers. Also..." Seiji pulled a cellphone out of his pocket and put it on top of the desk. "I sent a message to my friend Nishikido asking for that guy's address."

Natsume took the cellphone and checked. His expression changed, no doubt upon seeing the text from Nishikido.

"And…why did you kill him?"

"He had the dirt on me."

"The dirt…"

"Yeah…I'll explain in detail later. That guy came to my bar two days in a row and blackmailed me, saying he wanted to sleep with Kyoko. He said if I let him just once, he wouldn't say anything to the police, and he'd also hand over his proof. If he did tell the police, my future and my family were done for. I went home and got on my hands and knees to beg Kyoko. I asked her to sleep with that guy just once, no questions asked. I told her it was to protect me and our family—"

"So you asked Nishikido for that man's address, and you both visited him?"

"Yup. While he was with Kyoko, I wandered around nearby. But then I got worried about him not keeping his promise. Ohta was a sly bastard. I thought he might blackmail me over and over again. First it would be Kyoko's body, but next it would be money… I realized that he'd suck me dry and completely wreck my happy life. So I prepared to kill him, and waiting until Kyoko had left, I broke into his house and strangled him by his neck and killed him—"

"What dirt did he have on you?"

Seiji gazed into Natsume's eyes. "I attacked your daughter."

The moment he uttered the words, all emotion seemed to vanish from Natsume's eyes.

Seiji suffered the long silence that followed, watched by a pair of hollow eyes that could have been marbles.

"Why…" Natsume finally managed to utter.

"Your lectures irritated me. You said stuff like I couldn't just be consumed with hate. I could overcome any hardship if I had the strength? I was disgusted by you and the idealistic claptrap you kept spouting. Well, I thought, how about you faced a little hardship too. It's your own damn fault that your daughter is a vegetable—"

Seiji fanned Natsume's rage with his every word.

The more the man directed it at Seiji, the more likely he was to pin the murder—his mind muddled with hatred—on Seiji.

"That guy dared to blackmail me like he didn't have something to answer for himself. If he hadn't done that to me, he wouldn't have had to die… What an idiot, huh? I attacked your daughter and killed Ohta. Here's proof."

Seiji pulled a hair ornament from his pocket and threw it in front of Natsume. It was the one he'd taken from Emi back then.

After witnessing Natsume's tearful appeals on TV, Seiji thought to throw it away many times, but couldn't.

He couldn't forget the crime he'd committed. Beyond a doubt, he had struck an innocent girl in the head and stolen a precious thing from Natsume. The proof of his abyssal sin—

Gazing at the hair ornament, Natsume sat preternaturally still, as though his soul had been yanked out.

Worried, Nagamine peered at his partner from the back.

With a sluggish motion, Natsume took the hair ornament. He stood up unsteadily, turned his back to Seiji, and headed to the door with stumbling steps.

Nagamine followed him out of Interrogation Room Two.

Natsume was walking down the hallway with absentminded steps. Nagamine wanted to get to him immediately but couldn't leave Tsukamoto alone. He asked a detective in the investigation section across the corridor to switch with him before chasing after Natsume.

The man was sitting on a hallway bench, his hanging head in his hands.

"Are you okay?" Nagamine called out, but there was no sign

of a response.

He bent over next to Natsume and placed a sympathetic hand on the man's shoulder. It was shaking. Perhaps he was crying.

"We can leave the rest to someone else," Nagamine said, patting the shoulder.

Natsume slowly lifted his face. His bloodshot eyes on Nagamine, he shook his head.

"I know what she's hiding."

With those words, and as though summoning all his strength, Natsume stood up. He climbed up the stairs to the assembly hall on the third floor, went in, and headed to the desk with the computer. He opened a folder on screen and clicked the photos of the assailant case. Once they were printed out, he took them and left the hall.

"What is it that she's hiding?" Nagamine asked from behind, but Natsume continued on to the interrogation rooms without turning around. He went into Room 1.

When he sat at the desk across from Kyoko, she looked up in surprise again.

Natsume placed the photos in front of her. "You already knew, didn't you," he said.

Monitored by another detective, Seiji had his face turned to one wall.

He knew that Kyoko was in the adjacent room. No matter how hard he listened, however, he heard no sounds from next door.

His eyes fixed on one spot on the wall, he earnestly hoped that Kyoko was matching her story with his.

Seiji heard the door open and turned to face it. Nagamine and Natsume came in.

"Thank you," Natsume acknowledged, and the detective who'd been monitoring Seiji left the interrogation room. "And sorry to make you wait."

Seiji was facing Natsume across a desk once more. "How was it… Didn't Kyoko tell you the same thing? Whatever you say to her, she might still try to cover for me, though."

"She told us the truth."

The truth—

"She killed Toru Ohta."

"Are we still stuck on that? The one who killed Ohta was—"

"She was having sex with him for the last six months," Natsume interrupted.

"Six months…"

The words dealt an intense shock to Seiji. Kyoko had been in a physical relationship with Ohta for as long as half a year?

Then why had Ohta demanded that Kyoko sleep with him for just one night?

It made no sense, unless it was just to make Seiji suffer.

He recalled what Ohta had said then.

If you tell Kyoko that, I'll tell you something interesting—

If Seiji had asked Kyoko, did Ohta mean to tell him next that they'd been having an affair all along?

That would have completely severed any bond between Seiji and Kyoko.

But why would Kyoko be with Ohta for half a year—

"He had some dirt on her, too. He threatened her to do as he said if she didn't want you and her parents to know. She'd been coerced into that relationship."

"Dirt…"

"If you ever found out, Nozomi's happy family would crumble. Your relationship with her parents would crumble, too. No, not just that, her own relationship with her parents might crumble. She said that she wanted to take it back so much that she reluctantly slept with Ohta."

"Wait a second. Dirt…" Seiji had no idea what Natsume

meant. "What kind of secret did he have against her?"

"She knew. That you were the assailant—"

Seiji's head went blank.

"When you attacked my daughter, it wasn't just Ohta. She witnessed it, too."

That was impossible—

"Going home from cram school, they took a shortcut through the park and saw you in the middle of assaulting my daughter. It might have been because you were so upset, but you didn't notice running past her. She hadn't been able to report it because she liked you. After having failed to turn you in to the police, it was her younger sister Yasuko who was attacked and killed a week later, by the same culprit as far as the world knew. Then, you disappeared from sight. She wanted to believe you weren't the culprit in Yasuko's case, but the thought that you might be remained and tormented her. She couldn't share her suspicions with anyone. Doing so meant admitting that she hadn't reported your assault on my daughter. More than anything, the guilt was tearing her apart..."

"The guilt..."

"Over the fact that if she'd reported the first crime to the police, her sister wouldn't have been killed. A sense that she bore some of the blame for her sister's death... The thought haunted her. Then, when she was twenty, she met you again at a bar by chance. Just seeing your face set off her pent-up emotions, and she ran out crying."

Her tears back then hadn't been due to the overwhelming joy of being reunited with him.

But—

"Why...did she date me then..." Seiji muttered.

"I think her genuine affection for you was half of it. You didn't have anything to do with Yasuko's case. She prayed that was true. But the other half of it was that she wanted you to feel the pain all your life if you were indeed her sister's killer..."

Wanted him to feel the pain all his life—

"You'd probably never date her if you had attacked Yasuko knowing that she was Kyoko's sister. Since you did start seeing Kyoko, you must have attacked Yasuko unawares. Even so, it was unforgivable. The suffering the victims' families had been through... She wanted to make sure you were in close contact with her and her family for the pain it would inflict on you. She wanted you to dwell on the depth of your sin and to share their festering wound forever. She must have thought that becoming husband and wife and bearing constant pain, together, was how you two might do penance for her sister."

But...

Seiji's vision grew blurry.

So Kyoko hadn't agreed to become his wife out of pure love as he'd believed...

"Getting married to your sister's killer isn't an easy thing to understand. She must have been deeply conflicted. But going to such lengths to be with you isn't something that simply leaves me baffled. A victim's family doesn't just wish for the culprit to go to prison or to be punished severely, but to reflect on the crime and to continue to feel the pain... That is our wish."

"And that's why Kyoko was being threatened by Ohta? That's why she had to become his plaything?"

"That's right... Knowing you two were happily married, Ohta blackmailed her. He told her that if she didn't do as he said, he'd tell both you and her parents that she'd married you knowing that you were the attacker. Meanwhile, her life with you and Nozomi had turned into something irreplaceable for her. And of course there was her relationship with her parents. She could only do what he said. But that day, on the floor in Ohta's room... she found her sister's hair ornament. She killed Ohta, strangling his throat with a telephone cord, overcome by intense hatred.

She wanted to take home the accessory as evidence, but it was stuck in a gap between shelves and wouldn't come loose. While she was trying, she heard a noise downstairs. She said she gave up on taking home the ornament and slipped out of the house while you were searching the first floor."

It was actually the man who'd been having his way with her body who had killed her sister—

He remembered how Kyoko had come on to him that day. Finally sure that Seiji hadn't been the attacker in Yasuko's case, she'd wanted him from the bottom of her heart for the first time ever since they'd started dating. No doubt she was also thinking that she'd be separated from her family soon.

"A guy like that...deserved to die..." Seiji spat, wiping his tears away.

"Is that what you think?" Natsume asked quietly.

"Of course... Why, are you saying that you don't hate me?! Don't you want to kill me?!"

"You affirm hatred, and killing people you hate is fine. Is that what you want to teach Nozomi?!"

Natsume's words rang in Seiji's ears. It was the first time he'd heard the man shout.

"What her mother did was correct. Is that really what you want to teach Nozomi?!"

Seiji was speechless. He could only picture Nozomi's future in his mind's eye.

"When *my* daughter wakes up, that's not what I want to tell her. Even if she never wakes up...when we reunite in the next world, that's *not* what I want to tell her."

Seiji couldn't shake his own daughter's image from his head.

"The day you'll reunite with Nozomi probably isn't far away. What you want to tell her...what you need to tell her, the next time you see her..."

That was something he and Kyoko had to think over at length

and with all they had, Natsume's eyes seemed to contend.

"I am…sorry…"

Squeezing the words out from the bottom of his heart, Seiji doubled over on the desk and melt into tears.

Natsume stayed silent as Tsukamoto covered his face with both his hands and cried in front of them.

What was Natsume thinking now? What kind of expression was he facing Tsukamoto with? Looking at the man's back, Nagamine wondered.

"Please handle the rest," Natsume told him, then stood up slowly and exited the room.

Nagamine couldn't tell what the man was thinking even after glimpsing his profile.

Entrusting another detective with Tsukamoto, he went looking for Natsume. He tried the investigation section, with no luck. He walked down the hallway and asked a colleague who was nearby. Had he seen Natsume?

"Now that you mention it, he went up the stairs."

Only the practice room was up that way. Nagamine took the stairs, but Natsume wasn't there in the *dojo*, either. Nagamine went further up, to the roof.

When he opened the door, he saw Natsume's back. He appeared to be watching the sun set on the streets of Ikebukuro.

"So you were here," Nagamine said, approaching his partner.

Natsume turned around. "Good job."

Had the man been able to unload at least part of the burden he'd been carrying around for years? Or was he still afflicted with an open wound even after arresting his daughter's assailant?

It was hard to tell from his expression.

"What were you thinking about?" asked Nagamine.

"Well, nothing in particular…" Natsume replied, returning his gaze to the district of Ikebukuro. "When I'm done for the day,

I look at the streets from here. The hospital my daughter is in is over there… This is how I cheer myself up so I don't quit."

For me, investigations are always painful—

Nagamine recalled how Natsume had uttered those words.

He admitted that he was beginning to dig and respect Natsume as a detective. He also understood the pain a guy like Natsume faced by continuing to be a detective.

"Are you going to stay a cop?" Nagamine asked, at which his partner faced him. "You avenged Emi, if only a little. So now…"

Natsume shook his head. "Anything less than a world free of crime falls short of vengeance."

Transfixed by Natsume's gaze, Nagamine wondered if he'd ever felt so tense before.

The deep sorrow, and the powerful light that vied to counteract it, proved that Natsume's were unmistakably a cop's eyes.

About the Author

Contrary to the adjectives that would later come to be applied to his writing, Gaku Yakumaru, born in 1969 in Hyogo Prefecture, could not get enough of Steve McQueen and dabbled in musicals, screenplay writing, and comics scripting before winning the Edogawa Rampo Award for new mystery writers in 2005 with *An Angel's Knife*. A professional novelist ever since, he has won multiple nominations, including from the Mystery Writers of Japan, for his nuanced explorations of violent crimes perpetrated by minors and underage offenders' subsequent ethical choices. A few of his works, *An Angel's Knife* and *A Cop's Eyes* among them, have been adapted into TV dramas.

Begun in 2006, the *Cop's* series featuring Detective Natsume appears at a deliberate pace of roughly one magazine installment per year; the sequel, *A Cop's Promise*, was only collected in 2014. This English edition marks the phenomenal author's North American debut.

MORE MYSTERY FROM VERTICAL

Pro Bono
by Seicho Matsumoto
ISBN 978-1-934287-02-6, $14.95/16.95

From the father of postwar Japanese mystery who steered the genre away from locked rooms and toward a wider world of social forces, a classic about a young woman's revenge against a renowned lawyer.

City of Refuge
by Kenzo Kitakata
ISBN 978-1-934287-12-5, $14.95/18.95

It was only when the don of Japanese hardboiled came onto the scene in the '80s that the style truly became homegrown, weaning itself of anti-heroes with native names and foreign mannerisms.

Naoko
by Keigo Higashino
ISBN 978-1-932234-07-7, $14.95/19.95

Winner of the Japan Mystery Writers Award, this black comedy of hidden minds and lives turned the author, one of Japan's most ambitious and versatile mystery hands, into a perennial favorite.

KIZUMONOGATARI: Wound Tale
by NISIOISIN
ISBN 978-1-941220-97-9, $14.95/17.95

It doesn't get more cutting edge than this genre-traversing work by the palindromic mystery writer, the leading light of a younger generation who began their careers in the twenty-first century.

Learn more at www.vertical-inc.com